"Thank you," sh**"**

Her face was close. see the tears that sti skin was a lovely mocha and her lips were pink and inviting. He leaned forward. She stilled.

He bent his head and kissed her. She tasted like spaghetti sauce and red wine, sweet with just a hint of sharpness. And when she pulled back quickly, he had to force himself to let her go, to not demand more.

Her dark eyes were big.

"I hadn't planned on that," he said, proving that adult men lied, too. Maybe he hadn't exactly planned it, but for months, he'd been thinking about kissing Carmen.

She didn't answer. She just looked as shaken as he felt. A few more strands of her silky hair had fallen down, and her lips were trembling.

DEAD BY WEDNESDAY

BEVERLY LONG

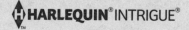

To my good friends, who have always believed it
was possible. Your support made the difference.
Now, please pass the wine.

Recycling programs
for this product may
not exist in your area.

ISBN-13: 978-0-373-74793-1

DEAD BY WEDNESDAY

Copyright © 2014 by Beverly R. Long

For questions and comments about the quality of this book,
please contact us at CustomerService@Harlequin.com.

Printed in U.S.A.

ABOUT THE AUTHOR

As a child, Beverly Long used to take a flashlight to bed so that she could hide under the covers and read. Once a teenager, more often than not, the books she chose were romance novels. Now she gets to keep the light on as long as she wants, and there's always a romance novel on her nightstand. With both a bachelor's and a master's degree in business and more than twenty years of experience as a human resources director, she now enjoys the opportunity to write her own stories. She considers her books to be a great success if they compel the reader to stay up way past their bedtime.

Beverly loves to hear from readers. Visit www.beverlylong.com, or like her at www.facebook.com/BeverlyLong.Romance.

Books by Beverly Long

HARLEQUIN INTRIGUE
1388—RUNNING FOR HER LIFE
1412—DEADLY FORCE**
1418—SECURE LOCATION**
1436—FOR THE BABY'S SAKE
1472—DEAD BY WEDNESDAY

**The Detectives

CAST OF CHARACTERS

Carmen Jimenez—She has helped hundreds of pregnant teenage girls, but she's worried that her own teenage brother is slipping away and that she'll lose him to gang violence, just like she lost her older brother. Is she willing to risk her heart and accept help from sexy and charming Detective Robert Hanson?

Robert Hanson—He's got his hands full trying to solve a serial murder case where the target is teenage boys. Still, wanting an opportunity to get to know Carmen better, he offers to spend time with her brother. When Carmen and her brother are suddenly missing, he knows that he must solve the case to save them both. However, time is running out.

Raoul Jimenez—Small for his age, he's a target for school bullies until a stranger befriends him and gives him the means to fight back. How far is he willing to go for revenge?

Frank Sage—He's upset about his daughter's pregnancy and he resents the help that Carmen is providing. Both his wife and his daughter are afraid of him. Should Carmen be more careful around the man?

JJ and Beau—Are they simply bullies or something much more dangerous? Will they be satisfied tormenting Raoul or are they interested in causing real trouble for Carmen?

Apollo—He's Raoul's mysterious new friend. Is he really looking out for Raoul or will he end up being the greatest danger of all?

Douglass Sparrow—A talented musician, frustrated with his lack of success. How many others will have to pay for his failures?

Chapter One

Wednesday

Robert Hanson looked up from his computer screen when Lieutenant Fischer approached his desk. He wasn't surprised or worried about the anger that flashed in his boss's eyes. He knew what had put it there. Had heard the news before he'd gotten off the elevator. Even though it wasn't his case, it had been enough to make him shove his half-eaten bagel back into the bag and toss his untouched orange juice into the nearest waste can.

"Got another dead kid," his boss said.

Robert had really, really hoped that the pattern would break. For the past three weeks, there had been a new dead kid every Wednesday morning. This was week four. "I heard," Robert said.

"Did you hear he was Alderman Franconi's nephew? His sister's kid."

Robert shook his head. Franconi was tight with the mayor. The heat was going to be turned up high. Not that every detective on the force wasn't already aware of the case and keeping his or her eyes open 24/7 looking for some kind of clue.

"Where's Sawyer?" his boss asked.

"On his way. He's dropping Liz and the baby off at Options for Caring Mothers."

"Okay." His boss started to walk away. Then stopped, turned and edged close to the metal desk. "Carmen Jimenez still work there?" he asked, his inquiry casual.

"I guess so," Robert said, working hard to keep his tone neutral. He hadn't seen Carmen since the wedding three months ago, where his best friend, Sawyer Montgomery, had married her best friend, Liz Mayfield. Robert had been the best man. Carmen had been the maid of honor. Her dress had been an emerald-green and it had wrapped around her body in a way that had made him break out in an instant sweat.

The groom had been calmer than he'd been.

Which was ridiculous because everybody knew that Robert Hanson never got rattled by a woman. He *managed* relationships. Not the other way around.

"Pretty woman," Lieutenant Fischer said.

Robert raised an eyebrow. The lieutenant had been married for twenty years and had kids in high school.

"Just making conversation, Hanson. If it's any

consolation, probably nobody but Sawyer and me realized that it was taking everything you had to keep your tongue from hanging out. We just know you better than most."

Robert shrugged and tried his best to look innocent. "I don't know what you're talking about, sir."

Lieutenant Fischer let out a huff of air. "Of course you don't. When Sawyer arrives, get your butts out to the scene. Blaze and Wasimole are still there. They could use some help talking to neighbors. Details are online in the case file."

Robert shifted in his chair and reached for his computer keyboard. But he let his hands rest on the keys.

Visions of Carmen Jimenez weren't that easy to push aside.

They'd danced, just once. It was expected, after all. And she'd felt perfect in his arms. And her scent had danced around him, making his head spin. He'd made small talk. *Nice wedding, wasn't it? Is your brother starting high school soon? Are you busy at work?*

She responded, her voice soft and sexy, with just a bare hint of a Spanish accent. *Very pretty. Yes, he is looking forward to playing in the band. Always lots to do.*

And when the music had ended, he hadn't wanted to let go. But she'd stepped away, murmured a quick thank-you and left him standing in the middle of the dance floor.

And later, when he'd tried to catch her eye, she'd looked away, and he wondered if it was deliberate. Toward the end of the evening, he hadn't had to wonder anymore. He'd finally worked up the courage to ask her to dance again and when she'd seen him approaching, had practically run into the ladies' restroom to avoid him.

He didn't need it written on the damn marquee. She wasn't interested. So he'd forgotten about her.

Right.

Well, he was working on it.

He tapped on his keyboard and brought up the case file. In their system, every entry was date- and time-stamped. Detectives Blaze and Wasimole, two veterans, had been on the scene within fifteen minutes of the call coming in at four o'clock this morning. Shortly after that, they'd entered a brief narrative into the electronic case file and updated it twice after that.

Victim had been discovered by a couple of sanitation workers. They hadn't touched the body. That was good. More than fifteen residents of nearby apartment buildings had already been interviewed and nobody had seen anything. That was bad.

There were multiple stab wounds, and fingers on his right hand had been severed and removed from the scene.

That wasn't a surprise.

The first victim had lost two fingers on his left hand. The second, two on the right. The third, two on his left hand.

Left, right. Left, right. There was a crazy symmetry about the handiwork but the end result was always the same. The kids were dead. Although it hadn't come easy. Coroner had determined in the first three deaths that the mutilation had occurred prior to death, which meant that they'd suffered the pain, then the blood loss; and finally the bastard had killed them by suffocating them by covering their noses with duct tape and stuffing a red bandanna in their mouths.

The killer hadn't bothered to remove the bandanna once the kids were dead.

Robert checked the notes. Yep. Victim had been found with his nostrils taped shut and a red bandanna stuffed in his mouth. He clicked on the pictures that had already been uploaded and started scanning them. They were gruesome and made his empty stomach twist.

When he heard Sawyer's footsteps, he was grateful for the interruption. His partner shrugged off his heavy coat, pulled out his desk chair and sank into it.

"You look like hell," Robert said.

"It's amazing the trouble one little tooth can cause," Sawyer said, his lazy drawl more pronounced than usual. "Catherine was up several times during the night. That doesn't happen very often."

"How's Liz?" Robert asked.

"Fabulous," Sawyer answered, sounding like a very happy man. "Although she wasn't too crazy about me giving Catherine my leather belt to chew on. That is, until she saw how well it worked."

"Southern tradition?" Robert asked.

Sawyer shook his head. "Midwest desperation."

Robert stood up. "Well, we got another kind of tradition going on here and quite frankly, it sucks." He pointed at his computer. Sawyer got up, rounded the desk, stood behind Robert, and quickly read through the information.

"Henry Wright," Sawyer said, resting his eyes on the text that had been added just an hour or so ago once the body had been identified.

"Alderman Franconi's nephew," Robert added. That wasn't in the notes.

"This is going to get interesting fast," Sawyer said.

"I know the area," Robert said. "Residential, mostly multiunit apartments. Some commercial."

Sawyer picked up the gloves that he'd tossed on his desk. He pulled them on. "Let's go knock on some doors. But take pity on me, for God's sake, and stop and get some coffee on the way. It's freezing out there."

"It's January in Chicago. What do you expect?"

"It would be nice if it got cold enough that all the killing stopped."

"It's cold," Robert said, "but I don't think hell has frozen over yet."

The two men piled into their unmarked car, with Robert driving. He pulled out of the police lot and five minutes later, found street parking in front of their favorite coffee shop. Once inside, he waited patiently while Sawyer had to flash a picture of six-month-old Catherine after the woman behind the counter asked for an update on the little girl.

Robert was damn happy for his friend. Liz was a great woman, and given how much she and Sawyer were enjoying their adopted daughter, Robert figured they'd be adding to their family in no time.

He wasn't jealous.

Hell, no. He had the kind of freedom that married men dreamed about.

Back in the car, he sipped his coffee, grateful for the warmth. It hadn't been above twenty degrees for two weeks, which meant that the four inches of snow that had fallen three weeks ago lingered on. Most of the roads were clear, but the sidewalks that hadn't been shoveled right away now had a thick layer of hard-packed snow, making walking dangerous.

It was dirty and grimy and very non-postcard-worthy. Even in the high-rent area known as the Magnificent Mile, things were looking a little shabby.

Ten minutes later, Robert left the car in a no-parking zone. Five feet away, the alley entrance was still blocked off with police tape. He looked around. When he'd been a kid, he'd lived just a few blocks from here. For a couple years, he and his mom and husband number three had shared an apartment in one of the low-income high-rise buildings. His mom still lived less than ten blocks away.

He'd spent a fair amount of time on these streets. The area still looked much the same. There were a couple small restaurants, a dry cleaner, a tanning salon and one of those paycheck advance places where the interest started doubling the minute your loan payment was late. There was a church a block down, and the neighborhood school was just around the corner.

Buses ran up and down these streets in the daytime, leaving the snow-packed sidewalks tinged with black exhaust.

Sawyer crushed his empty coffee cup. "Ready?" he asked, pulling the collar of his heavy coat tighter.

"Sure," Robert said. He tossed his empty cup over his shoulder into the backseat.

It wasn't hard to see where the body had been found. The hard-packed snow was an ugly combination of black soot and fresh blood. Detective

Charlene Blaze was talking to one of the evidence techs, who was still scraping the snow for something. He didn't see her partner, Milo Wasimole.

"Hey, Charlene," Robert said. "How's it going?"

She was a small woman, maybe mid-fifties. Her first grandchild had been born the previous week. Her face was red from the cold. "Okay, I guess. I lost feeling in my toes about a half hour ago."

"Lieutenant Fischer asked us to swing by."

She nodded. "Yeah, all hands on deck when an alderman's nephew gets it," she said, her tone sarcastic.

Robert understood. Hell, there were teenagers killed almost every night in Chicago. Most of the killings were gang-related. And nobody seemed to get all that excited about it.

But after week two, when it had become apparent that they might have a serial killer on their hands, the cases had started to get attention.

Week three, local newspapers had gotten hold of the story, noting the similarities in the killings. Two days later, they got television exposure, when the twenty-four-hour news channels picked it up. Then the dancing had started. Because nobody in the police department wanted it widely known that three kids were dead and they didn't have a clue who was responsible.

"Press been here yet?" Robert asked.

Charlene nodded. "Oh, yeah. Can't wait to see

tomorrow's headline." She nodded goodbye to the evidence tech, who was putting away his things. "I know you guys already have your own caseload but I have to admit, I'm appreciative of every set of eyes I can get. This is getting really creepy. Based on what we know at this point, this was a good kid. Fourteen. Just made the eighth-grade honor roll. Played the trumpet in the middle-school band."

Robert had read the files of the other three dead kids and knew they had similar stories. First victim had been thirteen. Second, fifteen. Third, fourteen. All male. All good students. All without known gang ties. "Any connection to the previous three victims?"

"No. All four lived in different parts of the city and went to different schools. We don't have any reason to believe they knew each other or had common friends."

Robert shook his head. "Nobody ever said it was going to be easy." He pulled his gloves out of his pocket. "Sawyer and I'll start knocking on some neighbors' doors. Maybe we'll get lucky and somebody saw something."

CARMEN JIMENEZ SWAYED back and forth with six-month-old Catherine on her hip. "I can't believe how big she's getting," she said to Liz, who was busy making coffee. "I saw her just a few weeks ago and she already looks different."

"I know. I'm almost grateful that her regular babysitter got sick. It's nice to bring her to work with me." Liz pushed the button on the coffee machine.

"Did Sawyer get her room finished?" Carmen asked.

Liz smiled. "It's gorgeous. I can't believe he had the patience to stencil all those teddy bears. You should come see it. We're getting pizza tonight. You and Raoul could join us."

"Raoul has band practice tonight. Even so..." She stopped.

Liz frowned at her. "What's wrong? You look really troubled."

"Nothing," Carmen denied automatically. Then remembered this was Liz, her best friend. "I was going to say that even so, he probably wouldn't want to come with me. I haven't said much, but I'm worried about Raoul."

"What's wrong with your brother?" Liz reached for Catherine and settled the little girl on her own hip.

"He's not talking to me. By the time I get home from work, he's already in his room. He comes out for dinner, shovels some food in, and retreats back to his cave. I'm lucky if I get a few one-word answers."

"He's an adolescent boy. That's pretty normal behavior. Aren't you almost thirty? That automatically makes you too old to understand anything."

"I know. It's just hard for me. It seems as if it was just weeks ago that he and his best friend Jacob were setting up a tent in our living room, laughing like a bunch of hyenas until the middle of the night."

"I can see why you'd miss that," Liz said with a smirk.

Carmen rolled her eyes. "I know, I know. But in the old days he couldn't wait to tell me what had happened at school." She swallowed. "He used to confide in me."

Liz wrapped her free arm around her friend's delicate shoulder. "That, my friend, is the difference between ten and fifteen. Give him a couple more years and he'll start talking again. In the meantime, you need something else to focus on."

"Maybe I'll take up knitting," Carmen said. "I couldn't find my scarf this morning."

Liz shook her head. "That's not what I was thinking."

Carmen sighed loudly. She and Liz had had this conversation. "I know what you were thinking."

"I never thought I'd play matchmaker. Really, I didn't. It's just that I'm so happy. I want that for you."

"I know. That's the only thing that's keeping me from tripping you on these stairs." She leaned forward and kissed Catherine's soft cheek. "Take care of your mother, darling. Her head is in the clouds."

Liz shook her head. "Just think about it, please. Maybe try the online thing?"

"Sure. I'll think about it. But right now, I have more pressing issues. I'm meeting my new client in fifteen minutes. Alexa Sage is sixteen, seven months along and lives at home with her parents, who have no idea that she's pregnant."

Liz nodded. "Winter clothes make it easier to hide a pregnancy, that's for sure." She took another step. "Will you come for pizza tonight? Please?"

"No need to beg. My middle name is carbohydrate. I'll be there." Carmen stopped at her office door, unlocked it, opened the door and immediately walked across the small space to pull open the heavy curtain on the lone window. Most days the sun offered some warmth but today, everything outside was gray. Wednesday. Hump day. By five o'clock tonight, the workweek would be more than half over. Although for the counselors who worked at Options for Caring Mothers, their workweeks didn't tend to be so carefully defined. Babies came at all times of the day or night, and none of the staff wanted their teenage clients to be alone at that time.

Alexa Sage arrived five minutes later. She wore a big black coat and jeans tucked into black boots. Her short hair was a white-blond and her pale skin was clear and pretty, with nicely applied makeup. Her eyes were green and wary.

"It's nice to meet you, Alexa," Carmen said, motioning for the girl to take a chair. "I hope you didn't get too cold getting here."

"I took the bus," she said. She sat but didn't take off her coat.

"Better than walking," Carmen said, keeping up the small talk. "I have a younger brother, and when I don't have early-morning meetings, I drop him and his best friend off at school."

"My mother doesn't work. She takes my sister and me to school every day. Picks us up, too. That's what Frank Sage wants."

"Stepdad?" Carmen asked, noting the use of the first name.

"Nope. His blood is my blood. Let me tell you, that has kept me up a few nights. He doesn't like it when I call him Frank. My mom thinks it's disrespectful, too."

"Do you say it to be disrespectful?"

"I say it because I can."

Maybe that's why she'd had sex. Because she could. And now she was in a heap of trouble. "How did you find out about Options for Caring Mothers?" Carmen asked.

"My counselor at school. She gave me an OCM brochure."

That was how many of their referrals came. "I'm glad that happened," Carmen said. "Did you tell her that you were pregnant?"

"I think the school nurse told her. I got sick a couple times at school. The nurse thought I had the flu and wanted to send me home. I had to tell her the truth."

"But you haven't told your parents?"

"No."

"Why not?"

Alexa chewed her lip. "My dad works in some little factory and he hates his job. He gets mad when my sister or I get a B. Says that if we're not careful, we're going to be trapped in some dead-end job. When he finds out that I'm going to quit school to take care of the baby, he's not going to be happy."

"So, you're planning on keeping your baby?"

The girl nodded.

"What about the father of the baby?"

This got a shrug. "He's a junior, too, so we're not, you know, getting married or anything, but he's cool with it."

"He hasn't told his parents?"

"There's only his mom. And no, we both agreed that we wouldn't say anything to anybody."

Alexa was mature, but was she mature enough to handle a child? "Have you considered adoption?" Carmen asked.

Alexa shook her head. "So that she can be raised by somebody like my parents? No, thanks."

Carmen nodded. Not much to say to that, was there? "Have you had any prenatal care?"

Alexa nodded. "At the health department. Everything is fine. I'm twenty-eight weeks. The baby is due April 15."

"How much longer do you think you can hide your pregnancy from your family?" Carmen asked.

"Probably not much longer. In a week, I have a family wedding. I'm not going to be able to wear a sweatshirt and baggy pants or my coat. I think the cat is going to be pretty much out of the bag."

"You should tell your parents before then," Carmen said.

"I know. That's why I'm here. Frank doesn't do so good with surprises. Goes a little crazy sometimes."

"What kind of crazy?" Carmen asked. "Crazy yelling or crazy something else?"

"When my mother hit a post with the fender of our car, he slapped her so hard that he split her lip."

Carmen felt sick.

"You were the counselor who helped my neighbor, Angelina. She said you were wonderful. I was hoping you could be there when I tell him."

Chapter Two

Raoul almost dropped his trombone when a skinny man stepped out of the dry cleaner's doorway, right into his path. His dark hair was slicked down on his head and pulled back into a short ponytail. His skin was really pale and he had gray eyes.

"Hi, there," the man said.

He was about six inches taller than Raoul, which basically wasn't all that tall. His shoulders were wide and he had on a really ugly plaid coat.

Raoul tried to step around him.

The man stepped with him, blocking his path.

"Hey, man," Raoul said. He'd already had a really bad day and all he wanted was to go home.

"Is that how you treat your friends, Raoul?"

Friends? "Who are you? How do you know my name?" Raoul asked, feeling uncomfortable. He looked around. There were other people on the sidewalk, but nobody seemed to be paying any attention to him.

"I know a lot about you. Your brother Hector and I were friends. Real tight."

Hector had been dead for eleven years. Whenever anybody said Hector's name, his sister, Carmen, got a real funny look on her face and she got sad. Once, when he asked her about it, she said that she was just so sorry that Hector had died.

That made him feel even worse that he couldn't remember Hector. He'd only been four when he'd died. He couldn't tell Carmen the truth. That would probably make her even sadder.

"You really knew Hector?"

"Oh, yeah. One time, before he died, he told me that if anything ever happened to him, that I should watch out for you."

Raoul didn't know what to say to that and anyway, his throat felt tight.

"Your brother used to talk about you all the time. Said that having a kid brother was cool."

Hector would have understood how hard it was to be the smallest kid in the class. He'd have known how humiliating it was to have someone jam your head into a toilet. He'd have known how ridiculous it felt to be tripped going down the hall and have your books fly everywhere.

He'd have known how much it hurt when everyone laughed.

"What's your favorite song?" the man asked, giving Raoul's shoulder a light punch.

Raoul didn't want to talk music. Even though this guy had been a friend of Hector's, he sort of gave him the creeps. "What's your name?" he asked again.

The man shook his head. "We'll talk soon, Raoul. I know what your brother wanted for you. I'm here to make sure you get it. Now, go home. Practice your music like a good boy."

BY THE END of the day, the police knew just a little more than they had that morning. The boy had not been killed on site. No, somewhere else, and then brought into the alley. One of the neighbors said that he'd left the neighborhood bar and walked home, cutting through the alley shortly before two in the morning. He swore that the body hadn't been there. If he was right, then the drop-off had occurred sometime between two and four, which was earlier than the other three killings. Those bodies had been found late in the day, and the coroner had estimated time of death to be late afternoon, early evening.

Was the killer getting more anxious?

That thought kept Robert and Sawyer and a half dozen other detectives knocking on doors, for six blocks in every direction, in the hopes that somebody had seen something. Maybe they'd also walked through the alley, maybe they'd seen a car idling nearby, maybe they'd heard something unusual.

It was the proverbial looking for a needle in a haystack, but dead kids got feet on the street.

Early evening, Robert and Sawyer returned to the parking lot behind their police station. They parked the department-issued cruiser and walked toward their own cars. "I'm starting to really hate Wednesdays," Robert said.

Sawyer nodded. "Yeah, me, too. At least I have dinner to look forward to. I'm picking up pizza at Toni's. Liz invited Carmen over to look at Catherine's room. I painted it this weekend."

All damn day Carmen Jimenez had been on his mind. "I've been thinking of doing some painting," Robert said.

Sawyer smiled. "Yeah. But for some reason, I doubt you're thinking pink."

Robert shrugged. "What did you use? A gloss, semigloss or a flat?"

Sawyer waved a hand. "I have no idea. I used the paint in the can that Liz brought home from the paint store."

"Oh, good grief. Now I've got to see this paint job. If you get the pizza, I'll get a couple bottles of wine on my way. As long as you think it will be okay with Liz."

"Liz adores you. Why, I'm not a hundred percent sure."

Robert shoved his friend, then had to grab him to keep him from slipping on the snow, which was gathering a top layer of ice as the temperature continued to drop.

"Be careful," Robert said.

"Be on time," Sawyer said, getting into his car. "I'm hungry."

Less than forty-five minutes later, Robert knocked on his partner's door. He'd had time to run home, take a five-minute shower and grab a couple of bottles of wine off the rack in his kitchen.

While he was perfectly happy in his ultramodern high-rise, he had to admit that he loved Sawyer's house. A month before Liz and Sawyer had gotten married, Liz and Catherine had moved into the eighty-year-old brownstone. Now the family occupied the first two floors and rented out the top floor to a single woman who spent most of the week traveling.

The house had good bones. Before meeting Liz, Sawyer had already refinished the oak floors, replaced all the lighting and hung artwork that reminded him of the Deep South. Liz had added feminine touches that had turned the wonderful structure into a home.

"Hi, Robert," Liz said as she opened the door. She leaned forward for a kiss on the cheek. "Come in quickly. It's freezing."

He stepped inside, closing the door behind him. He could hear the soft murmur of voices from the living room. He heard Carmen laugh, and there wasn't a cold bone in his body.

Liz peered at the wine. "Very nice," she said. "The pizza is good but this may put it to shame."

Robert set the wine on the entryway table, shrugged off his coat, stuffed his gloves in one pocket and handed it to Liz. She hung the coat in the hall closet. There was a royal-blue cape hanging there and he suspected it belonged to Carmen.

It was crazy but he liked seeing his coat next to hers.

He picked up the wine and followed Liz into the family room. Like any good cop, he took in the details quickly. Fireplace was lit. Soft jazz played in the background. Catherine lay on her back, on the very nice rug that had been one of Liz's contributions to the house. Both plump little legs were moving, as if she were pedaling an invisible bicycle. Sawyer was stretched out next to her.

Carmen was sitting in the chair, leaning forward, looking at the baby. The light from the fireplace cast a soft glow around her. She wore a red sweater and black slacks. Her long dark hair flowed over her shoulders.

She was beautiful.

And when she turned, he saw that she wasn't surprised to see him. Her face was composed, polite. And he should have felt much the same. After all, he'd known that she was going to be here. That was why he'd wheedled an invitation with some crazy excuse that he was interested in paint. Paint, for God's sake. It was ridiculous.

And it was pretty damn ridiculous, too, that just looking at Carmen made him feel short of breath and a little unsteady on his feet.

"Hi," she said.

"Hi," he managed.

Sawyer sat up. "Cold beer in the fridge."

Robert nodded. "I'll stick with this," he said, holding up the wine. He looked at Carmen. "Can I get you a glass?"

She nodded. "Yes, thank you."

Liz reached for the wine. "I'll get some for both of you. I need to check the pizza anyway. We put it in the oven to keep it hot." She took a step. "Have a seat, Robert," she said gently.

He sat. And felt like an awkward sixteen-year-old at his first prom. His shirt felt too tight and his heart was racing in his chest.

The only noise in the room was Catherine's happy squeals. Carmen stared at the fire. He stared at the antique umbrella stand in the corner of the room.

Sawyer looked from Carmen to him and back again. Finally, his friend sprang to his feet. He reached for Catherine and cupped her in the crook of his elbow. "Liz probably needs my help in the kitchen," he said as he left the room.

Now there was just silence.

Sawyer had probably been gone for less than a minute when Carmen turned her head. "I don't think Liz really needs his help."

He relaxed. "Maybe if we were having grits and chicken-fried steak."

"Ugh," she said with a smile that made her even prettier. "I'd suddenly have to run an errand."

"I'd drive you," he said. "Although to be fair, the man makes a great gumbo. He brought some into work one day, and it made me nostalgic for my last trip to the French Quarter."

"I think I'd love New Orleans," she said. "Maybe someday."

The kitchen door swung open, and Liz emerged holding two wineglasses. "Follow me," she said, leading them to the dining room. There was a huge pizza in the middle of the table with a big bowl of salad next to it. Sawyer was clipping Catherine's high-chair tray on.

They sat, and Catherine immediately started squealing and pounding her plump fists on the high-chair tray. Liz smiled apologetically. "Sorry. This is the kind of ambience we have now."

Robert dished out a slice of pizza and handed it to Carmen. "No problem. Table manners like her father."

They were done with their pizza and cutting into the cheesecake that Carmen had picked up at the bakery after work when Robert's phone buzzed with an incoming text message. He glanced at it, shook his head and turned his phone upside down on the table. "Sorry about that," he said.

"Bad news?" Liz asked.

"A reporter from the newspaper," he explained. "She's evidently not getting enough of a story from Blaze and Wasimole, so she tracked me down. I imagine she got the number from one of the people we talked to today. We generally leave a card in case they think of something that might be helpful."

"These killings are the only thing the local talk show hosts were discussing today," Liz said. "It's getting very scary."

It was horrible, thought Carmen. With Raoul being about the same age as the other victims, it made her sick to hear people talking about the stories. Her heart ached for the terrible loss that the families had suffered, for the pain the boys had endured. "I didn't know if I should say anything to Raoul," she admitted. "I didn't want to scare him unnecessarily but I also didn't want him to be naive."

"Where did you land on it?" Robert asked.

"I left the newspaper on the table one morning, folded so that he could easily see the headline. He read the story and that gave me the opportunity I was waiting for. I tried to gently suggest that it was important to be careful, to always be watching."

"What did he say?" Liz asked.

Carmen rolled her eyes. "He said, and I quote, 'Sis. There are three million people in the city of Chicago. Eight million if you count the suburbs. I don't think anybody is looking for me.' I didn't push it. I'm crazy enough about other things, like brushed teeth and pants that stay up around his waist."

"Raoul's such a smart kid.. You didn't need to say anything else," Liz said. "He gets it."

"Yeah, and we're going to *get* this guy," Sawyer said, his tone confident. "He's going to make a mistake. In fact, he already has."

"What's that?" Liz asked.

"He mutilates and suffocates his victims. That's been reported in the press. What hasn't been reported is that the victims have all been found with red handkerchiefs in their mouths. We've been successful in keeping that out of the press. But that shows an arrogance on his part—that he's so confident that he won't be caught that he can afford to leave clues at the scene. Arrogance makes criminals sloppy."

"Can you trace the handkerchiefs?" Carmen asked.

"We've tried. No luck so far," Robert said. "They're sold in a bunch of stores. But something will break, soon. It has to." He leaned across the table and tickled Catherine's belly. "Right, darling?"

She giggled, breaking the tension at the table.

Carmen felt more relaxed than she had in months. That wasn't how she'd expected the evening to go. She'd gotten to Liz's house and her friend had quickly pulled her aside. *Sawyer just told me he invited Robert, too. Are you okay with that?*

Heck no, she wasn't okay with that. She'd met Robert Hanson just weeks before Catherine was born, when Catherine's mother was kidnapped by a gang leader who wanted to steal the baby. Robert had been a little brash, maybe even a little cocky, but he'd been helpful to both Liz and Sawyer.

And she had tried to ignore that whenever he was close, it seemed a little harder to focus. She'd done pretty well with that until the wedding and then the dance.

Robert Hanson knew how to hold a woman. For a big man, his touch had been light and his steps graceful.

But she'd known that he was a man who knew what to do. And her skills were rusty. Real rusty. She was twenty-nine years old and hadn't been on a date in thirteen years.

No worries, she'd assured her friend. After all, they'd had one little dance. She remembered it but he'd probably forgotten it the next day. She told herself it was silly to think for even one minute that the evening would be the least bit awkward.

But when the door opened and she heard his voice in the foyer, her senses had become more acute. She felt her skin get warm and knew it had nothing to do with Sawyer's nice fireplace.

And she'd tried to remember that it was just a DWF night. Dinner With Friends. They'd have a little pizza, some wine, a few laughs.

And she'd prayed that the butterflies in her stomach would get the message.

She'd worried for nothing. Robert Hanson, in his usual charming way, had made the night perfect.

Now that they'd finished with their cheesecake, Robert pushed back his chair and began to gather up the dirty plates. Liz started to get up. "I've got this," he said. "I'm anxious to see the paint job that your husband did. I must admit, he's never impressed me as being all that artistic."

Sawyer wadded up his cloth napkin and threw it at Robert. "If I get tired of wrestling with the bad guys, maybe I'll start my own painting business."

"Not a chance, Michelangelo," Robert said. "You're not leaving me on my own."

Liz shook her head. "Like either of you would ever stop being cops. Come with me."

They followed Liz back to Catherine's room. It

had been painted a pale mint-green. Waist-high was a border of dancing teddy bears in yellows and pinks.

"It's adorable," Carmen said. "Very impressive. Can I hire you? My kitchen desperately needs paint."

Sawyer smiled and shook his head. "I don't want to see another stir stick for quite some time. Robert, you seemed to know a lot about painting earlier."

"I work cheap," Robert said, his tone casual.

"I'll keep that in mind," Carmen said, grateful to get out of the conversation so easily. The idea of sexy Robert Hanson in her kitchen, face smeared with paint, looking all adorable, had the butterflies double-timing it. Her stomach lining was getting scratched. "I should probably get going," she added.

Sawyer and Robert grabbed coats out of the closet and Carmen hugged her friend. "Thank you so much. Everything was delicious. Remember, I'm going to be late tomorrow."

"Be careful, okay?" Liz replied, her tone serious.

Both Sawyer and Robert immediately stopped their conversation. "What's going on, honey?" Sawyer asked, moving close to his wife.

"Carmen has a new client. Unfortunately, the girl hasn't told her parents that she's pregnant. She's afraid to. Dad evidently has a history of a violent temper. Anyway, she asked Carmen to be there when she breaks the news."

Robert took a step forward. "He's coming to OCM?"

"No," Carmen said. "That won't work. The minute she tells him that she wants to meet him at a pregnancy counseling center, he's going to have a pretty good idea of what's going on."

"You're not going to this guy's house?" Robert asked, his tone challenging.

Carmen shook her head. "No. I'm not that crazy," she said, trying to make light of it. She saw that it wasn't working. "Frank Sage evidently stops for coffee every morning at a little place on the corner of Taylor and Minx. His daughter and I are going to meet there and uh, break the news. It's a public place where he'll probably feel inclined to behave. It was the best plan I could come up with."

Robert was frowning at her. "You do this kind of thing often?"

"Not often, but I've had cases where we've had to quickly remove a young girl from a situation when her parents or her boyfriend or somebody else couldn't handle the news of the pregnancy. We need to protect our clients and their babies."

"You think that's what's going to happen here?" Robert asked.

"I don't know. I should be able to tell. If I have

any reason to believe that he's going to harm my client physically, I'll take the necessary steps."

Liz stepped in and wrapped an arm around Carmen's shoulder. "She's little but she's tough. I'll see you tomorrow," she said. "Be careful driving home."

She and Robert left. She saw a red SUV parked behind her car. She assumed it was Robert's. "Well, good night," she said when they got to her car.

"It's pretty late," he said. "How about I follow you?"

Was Robert Hanson asking to be invited in? The idea was absurd. And terribly exciting. She felt sixteen again. "I drive all the time at night," she said.

"That doesn't make it a good thing. Please let me do this."

Liz had always said that both Sawyer and Robert were real gentlemen. "Okay. Do you need my address?" she asked. "In case you lose me at a light?"

He shook his head and smiled. "I won't lose you."

And he didn't. She drove a sedate thirty-eight miles an hour and he stayed a couple car lengths behind her. The whole time she worried about what she should say if he asked to come in. When she parked at her apartment building, she still didn't have an answer.

He pulled up next to her.

"What floor?" he asked.

"Second. That window is my kitchen," she said, pointing at the end of the building closest to them.

"Okay. Flip the light twice and I'll know you're in safe. Have a good night, Carmen."

"Uh…sure. Thanks." She practically ran into the building. She got inside her apartment and pressed herself up against the hard wall. Her heart was pounding in her chest, and she didn't think it was from the physical exertion.

Then she remembered to flip the light twice.

Robert Hanson wasn't interested in coming inside, and she was a fool to think so.

Chapter Three

Thursday

Carmen was just slipping on her shoes the next morning when she heard Raoul's door slam. "You're up early," she said, ruffling his hair as he walked past her.

He didn't answer. Just went to the cupboard and pulled out a box of cereal. He poured a big bowl, added milk, grabbed a spoon from the drawer and stood at the counter. "I have band practice this morning," he said with his mouth full.

She ignored the poor manners. Lately, Raoul hadn't offered much conversation; she wasn't inclined to shut him down. "Practice before and after school?"

"Winter concert is next Thursday," Raoul said. "Mr. Raker said we better improve fast or we're going to be an embarrassment to ourselves and our families."

Carmen smiled. Mr. Raker could get a little

over-the-top sometimes. "You'll pull it off. I know you will."

"I guess." He chewed. "Hey, Carmen. Did Hector have a lot of friends in high school?"

Hector. He'd been two years older and in every way possible, her hero. And then he'd made a few bad decisions that changed the course of his life. All their lives, really.

And then he'd died.

"I guess," she said. Raoul never talked about Hector. "Why do you ask?"

He stared at her and put his half-eaten cereal down. "He was my brother. Can't I ask about my brother?"

"Of course," she said. "It's just…you surprised me, that's all. What would you like to know?"

He grabbed his coat. "Never mind," he said. "I have to go. It's Mrs. Minelli's turn to drive. She's probably already here."

"Raoul," she said.

A slamming door was her answer.

"Say hi to Jacob," she said, her voice trailing off at the end. She sank down on one of her kitchen chairs. Over the years, she'd had a few clients who were as young as fourteen or fifteen, but girls were different. They communicated. Boys just shut down.

It was driving her crazy.

She turned the lights off, grabbed her coat and

patted her pockets to make sure she had gloves. She normally drove to work, but she knew that parking near the coffee shop would be hard to find. It was easier to take a cab.

When she was just a few blocks away, she texted Alexa's cell phone. *Are you there?*

The response came almost immediately. *No. Five minutes.*

Carmen checked her watch. Alexa's father stopped in on his way to work. Same time, every day. He was due in ten minutes.

The cab stopped, and she handed over a ten and got out. She considered waiting outside for Alexa but across the street, the flashing sign on the bank indicated it was ten degrees.

And in Chicago, the wind never stopped blowing. Which made the windchill about twenty below.

She opened the coffee shop door, took her place in line and studied her choices. When it was her turn, she ordered a large hot chocolate and a glass of water. Then she turned to find a table.

And saw him.

Robert Hanson.

He smiled at her and held up his own cup. "Morning, Carmen. They make a great cup of coffee here, don't they?"

He looked fresh and handsome and as delicious as one of the scones in the front display case. "This is not your coffee shop," she hissed.

"I drink coffee all day long, all over the city. Why not here?"

She rolled her eyes. "Look, there's no need for you to be here. Everything is going to be fine."

"Good. Then you can just ignore that I'm here."

Robert Hanson was six-two and two hundred pounds of muscle. His eyes were a brilliant blue, his bone structure was strong and his thick light brown hair looked as if a woman had just run her fingers through it.

He was hard to ignore.

"Do not interfere," she said.

"As long as Dad behaves, that shouldn't be a problem."

Carmen shook her head and took the table in the corner. She turned her chair so that she could see the door but not Robert. She concentrated on taking deep breaths. When she felt she had it under control, she took small sips of her hot chocolate.

Alexa came in, wearing the same big, dark coat. The young girl got a cup of coffee and headed for Carmen. "I'm sorry I'm late. He should be here really soon."

"No problem." Carmen decided that now wasn't the time to lecture on the evils of pregnancy and caffeine. "When he arrives, make eye contact and motion him over to the table. Then I'll introduce myself and let him know that you have something that you'd like to tell him. Just be calm. It's going to be okay."

"You don't know my dad," Alexa said. She looked tired, as if she hadn't had much sleep.

Carmen reached over to pat the girl's hand but stopped when the teen stiffened in her chair. Carmen turned and immediately saw the resemblance between daughter and father. Their coloring was the same; the nose, too. Frank Sage was a big man, probably at least six feet. He wore gray work pants and a big black coat that hinted at a well-fed stomach. His blond hair was thinning on top.

He was frowning at his daughter.

Alexa motioned and the man hesitated. Then he walked across the room, bumping into a chair on the way.

"Alexa, what are you doing here?" he asked. He had a deep voice, somewhat raspy, likely from years of cigarettes. Carmen could smell smoke on his jacket.

"Hi, Dad," Alexa said.

Carmen stood up. She did not like him towering over her. She extended her hand. He stared at it. "Mr. Sage, I'm Carmen Jimenez. I am a counselor and I've been working with your daughter."

When it didn't appear that he was going to return the shake, Carmen dropped her arm. "Will you please have a seat?" she asked.

The man hesitated, then sat on the edge of his

chair. "A counselor? Working with my daughter," he repeated. "What the hell is this about, Alexa?"

Carmen sat down. "Alexa has something that she wants to tell you, Mr. Sage. And this is difficult for her. It may also be difficult for you to hear. All I'm asking is that you hear her out, give her a chance."

The man nodded. His eyes were narrowed.

"Dad." Alexa stopped and licked her lips. "I'm pregnant."

The man's face turned red. He shook his head. "No," he said, staring at his daughter.

Alexa nodded. "I'm going to have a baby around April 15."

"No," he repeated, his voice louder, as if by proclaiming it so, he could simply get the problem to disappear.

Alexa's face turned pink and she looked quickly around the coffee shop. A few people in line were staring in their direction. "Please, Dad. Carmen is a counselor at Options for Caring Mothers, a pregnancy counseling center. She's helping me."

The man swiveled in his chair, looked at Carmen, then stood up fast, catching the edge of the table. Cups and water glasses flew. Carmen felt the hot splash of liquid on her face and heard Alexa yelp. She looked up to see Frank Sage's big red face coming toward her.

ROBERT WRENCHED THE man's arm behind his back, put pressure on the back of his knees with a well-placed foot, and in seconds, had him facedown on the tile floor.

He looked around the room. "My name is Detective Robert Hanson. I'm a police officer with the Chicago Police Department. I need all of you to remain calm and to stay in your seats. I repeat, remain calm and stay in your seats."

He turned to look at Carmen. She was standing up. Her mouth was open and she looked shell-shocked. There was hot chocolate on her blouse, and some had splashed on her face and hair. He tightened his grip on Sage's arm, pulling it just a little higher. "Are you okay?" he asked her.

She nodded and turned to look at the girl who had also stood up. "Alexa?" She wrapped an arm around the girl's shoulder.

"I told you," the young girl said, her tone soft. She was looking at her dad.

There was a disgusting combination of hot chocolate, coffee and water pooling on the table. The uneven slate floor was causing a small trickle to drip off the side.

A helpful server walked by and offered Carmen a towel. Robert shook his head. "Leave it," he said. He wanted pictures.

Robert leaned close to the man's ear. He spoke

quietly. "If you didn't hear it the first time, my name is Detective Robert Hanson, with the Chicago Police Department. I'm going to let you get up, Mr. Sage. But if you make one wrong move toward your daughter, Ms. Jimenez, me or anybody else in this room, you're going to be in even bigger trouble than you are now. Do you understand?"

He waited until the big man nodded. Then he loosened his grip and let the man get to his knees. He kicked a chair toward him. "Sit there," he ordered.

The man did as he was instructed. His face was red and his eyes were wild, but he didn't try anything. He did not look at Alexa or Carmen.

Robert moved behind him. Quietly but distinctly, he read him his Miranda rights.

The man let him finish and then immediately said, "I didn't do anything wrong."

He'd had his arms up, coming toward Carmen, and if Robert hadn't been there to stop him, Carmen's injuries would have been far worse than some splashes with a hot drink. It was taking everything he had not to punch the son of a bitch.

"You caused hot liquid to land on Ms. Jimenez. That's battery, Mr. Sage. And by virtue of your size, your proximity and your aggressive posture, I'm adding criminal threatening to the list of charges."

Frank Sage said nothing. Then he looked at his

daughter. "I didn't mean to upset the table. I caught it with my legs. And I wouldn't have hurt her. I was…surprised. You surprised me. This wasn't the way it should have happened. Not with some stranger here."

Alexa stared at her hands.

Carmen stepped forward. "No closer," Robert said.

She nodded and sat down. "I believe Mr. Sage when he says that he didn't purposefully lift the table. And I'm sure we did catch him by surprise this morning with some very difficult news. If Mr. Sage feels that he can now have a reasonable conversation, I think we should forget the last five minutes and move forward. Alexa has a lot of decisions she needs to make and she needs her father's help." She motioned for Alexa to take her seat again.

No, Robert wanted to yell. In his head, he could still see Sage lunging over the table, his big hands ready to wring Carmen's neck.

"Please," Carmen said, looking at him. "Robert?"

Damn. Like he was going to be able to deny her anything. He squatted next to Frank Sage. "You're lucky. She's a nice person. I'm not that nice, in case you were wondering." He pulled a business card out of his pocket and handed it to Sage. "Take this, as a little reminder that I'm going to be watching you."

He stepped back and watched while Carmen used the towel to sop up enough of the liquid to keep more from hitting the floor. Then, the three of them conversed for a few minutes. She talked and Alexa and Sage listened. Then it was Alexa's turn. Sage said very little. After a few minutes, Carmen stood up. She extended a hand to Sage. He hesitated, then extended his own arm, giving her hand a quick shake. Then he left without a backward glance at the two women.

Alexa stood up next, hugged Carmen, said something that made Carmen smile and then left. Carmen finally looked at him.

She was sitting at a dirty table, a large splotch of brown liquid on her pink shirt, with more on her face and in her hair, and he'd never seen anyone more beautiful.

He moved over to the table. "You're sure you're okay?" he asked.

She looked down at her shirt. "Oh, yeah. This is the look I was going for." With two fingers, she rubbed at the sticky substance on her face. "By the way," she said, "thank you. I mean it. I know I wasn't very gracious about you being here but you were a big help."

He nodded. "What's next for Alexa and her parents?"

"They're going to tell her mom tonight. Alexa didn't want to tell her first because she was afraid that her father would be mad at her mom, thinking that she'd been hiding information from him. This way, he'll see how surprised his wife is by the news. Then they'll have to start talking about next steps. Alexa is determined to have this baby and take care of it. She probably could do it by herself, but it would be a whole lot easier if she had her parents' help."

"And where do you come in?"

"I'll continue to work with her throughout the remainder of the pregnancy and then after delivery, too. There are resources available to both her and her baby that I can help her with."

"Sage didn't look happy."

"He's not. Hopefully he'll work himself into the stage of acceptance. If he can't, then I'll help Alexa with finding a new place to live. I'm not going to let her live with somebody who can't get over his anger."

"I don't want you to ever go to their house," he said.

She narrowed her dark brown eyes. "Detective, I'm must have heard that wrong because it sounded as if you were telling me how to do my job."

He shook his head and rolled his eyes. "Come on, I'll walk you to your car. I assume you're going to want to go home and change."

She nodded. "Yes, but no car. I took a cab."

He frowned at her. "I'm not going to let you

stand around in a wet shirt when it's freezing, waiting for a cab. I'll drive you home."

He could tell she wanted to argue, but her shirt was probably uncomfortable enough that it changed her mind. "If it's no trouble."

Carmen Jimenez had been causing him trouble since the first day that he'd seen her. She'd been standing outside OCM, waiting while bomb specialists removed an explosive device that had been left on her boss's desk. He'd taken one look and his world had changed. His sleep was disturbed, he rarely got through a day without thinking of her and his sex life had taken a turn down a dead-end road. He still dated, made himself pretend that he was having fun, but he hadn't slept with anybody since that morning.

And she had barely given him the time of day.

If Sawyer or their boss knew that he was such a fool, Robert would never hear the end of it.

"No trouble," he said.

ROBERT DROVE WITH an ease and competence that impressed Carmen. She'd grown up in the city and had been driving in it for years, but all the traffic still made her nervous. Raoul had been hinting that he was going to get to take driver's education soon and that he'd need lots of practice hours. The thought of it made her ill. But she would do it. She would do anything for Raoul.

She pulled her cell phone from her purse, intending to check in with Liz. There was a missed call and a voice mail. She didn't recognize the number.

She listened to the voice mail and felt sick. She played it again. Then let her phone drop back into her purse.

"What's wrong?" Robert asked, checking his rearview mirror.

There was no reason to tell him. She'd been handling things on her own for a long time. She'd handle this, too.

"Carmen?" he said, his voice soft. "Was that Sage?"

She was so tired of being strong and so damn worried about Raoul. "That was Raoul's homeroom teacher. She wanted me to know that Raoul is failing two of his classes. He rarely turns in homework and on the last essay test, over half of his answers were wrong."

Robert nodded. "Is he a pretty good student, usually?"

"He's always made the honor roll. Oh, my gosh, I've never gotten a call like this. Never dreamed I'd get one."

"So talk to him. You're good at that," Robert said with an encouraging smile.

Carmen chewed on the corner of her lip. "It's not just the grades. There's something else going on but I have no idea what it is. He's changing. Right in front of my eyes. He won't talk to me. It's as if he doesn't even like me."

Robert slipped the car into a parking place in front of her apartment, shut it off and turned toward her. "Look, take it from somebody who used to be a boy," he said with a smile. "It's tough being a freshman in high school. He likes you. He just doesn't know how to show it."

"That's what Liz says."

"She's right."

Carmen shook her head. "I know Raoul better than I know anybody. It's been just the two of us for a long time. Our older brother, Hector, died when I was eighteen and Raoul was barely four. About a year later, our parents were killed in a car accident. I raised Raoul from that point."

"You were really just a kid yourself. That was a big responsibility you took on."

"I guess. It never entered my mind to do anything different. I was in college by then. We both did our homework at the kitchen table," she said, smiling at the memory.

"Good bonding time," Robert said.

She nodded. "I know him as well as I know myself. That's how I know that there's something else going on here. I just have to figure it out before it's too late." She swallowed hard. "Hector was shot by a rival gang member. He had just turned twenty." She closed her eyes for just a second, then opened them and looked at him. "I can't lose an-other brother. I just can't."

"You lost a great deal in a short period of time. Yet you went on, made a good life for yourself and your brother. It could not have been easy."

He seemed so sincere in his praise. She hadn't told him to impress him. She'd just wanted him to understand.

"I'll figure something out," she said, trying to change the subject.

"I could talk to him," Robert said.

It was a nice offer but it wouldn't work. "He doesn't know you. He's not going to trust you."

Robert shrugged. "Okay. So I get to know him. Invite me over for dinner tonight. I'll pick some-thing up on my way—maybe Chinese?"

"That's impossible," she blurted out.

"Okay. No Chinese. Italian? Although we just had pizza," Robert said.

He was deliberately misunderstanding her. "I'm sure you have better things to do than have dinner with a paranoid twenty-nine-year-old and a snarl-ing teenage boy." When Liz had first started dat-ing Sawyer, she'd confided that Robert was a bit of playboy.

"You're not paranoid, and unless he's rabid, I can take a little snarling from a fifteen-year-old."

"I don't know why you'd want to do this," Car-men said, shaking her head.

"Come on. It's my version of community service," he said easily. "You're not going to deny me the opportunity for that, are you?"

Chapter Four

From Carmen's apartment, Robert drove directly back to the police station. When he got there, he saw that Alderman Franconi was in Lieutenant Fischer's office. The door was closed, but the blinds were open just enough that Robert and every other person in the squad room understood that Alderman Franconi wasn't happy.

He made eye contact with Sawyer, who was sipping on a cup of coffee and eating some kind of pastry. He had a newspaper spread out on his desk. The headline said it all. Police Frustrated with Lack of Progress.

Frustrated? Oh, yeah.

As was the alderman, who spent another three minutes in the lieutenant's face before turning and leaving. When he walked through the squad room, he didn't look at or talk to anyone. Once he was out of the room, all heads turned toward the lieutenant's office. The man was standing in the door, not looking any worse for wear. It would take more than a frustrated alderman to rattle him.

"Well," Lieutenant Fischer said, his tone dry. "As you may have gathered, Alderman Franconi wants us to find the killer and string him up at Daley Plaza. Or we'll all be looking for new work."

Nobody reacted to the last line. It was this particular alderman's style to threaten jobs. He did it when the crowd control at the summer festivals didn't go well. He was certainly going to do it now. The alderman was a jerk about most things. He did have a dead nephew, however, so everybody was more inclined to cut him some slack.

Robert didn't have to have family to understand family. It had just been his mom and him, with a progression of husbands and live-ins over the years. His mom had been married five times, no, make that six. He sometimes forgot number four. That one had lasted less than six months. One had continued on for five years but Robert was convinced that was because the man was an over-the-road trucker and gone most of the time. That was actually the one guy he'd liked.

The weird thing was, his mother wasn't a bad person. People generally liked her. She was the life of the party. Had a good sense of humor, knew how to tell a joke. She drank too much, perhaps. But she was a pleasant drunk, not a mean one. She mostly made bad choices. Because she couldn't stand being without a man, couldn't stand being alone. And so whatever loser came along got credit for having testosterone, and was immediately a viable prospect.

Robert had been three when his biological dad had been killed in a car accident. His mother, who had been a beautiful woman with her blond hair and green eyes, had remarried within the year, although Robert didn't even remember that guy.

Now, if he felt inclined to ever look back, which he did not, the only way he could keep the parade straight in his head was to go to the pictures that his mother had stuffed in a shoe box. Every year, on his birthday, she'd taken a picture. And the man of the hour had always been in one of the shots.

None of them had been inclined to adopt him, or maybe his mother had never wanted that. He wasn't sure. From a very early age, before he even knew what the word meant, he'd considered them boarders in his home. There but not important. Certainly not family.

Her latest husband was retired military. He wore black shoes that always had a nice shine and he grew orchids in the small garden behind their house. His name was Norman. She called him Normie.

The man didn't say much when Robert visited. But then again, getting a word in edgewise was a feat when his mother was revved up. As Sawyer would say, she could talk the ears off a chicken.

Robert sat down at his desk and was surprised

to see two pink message slips in Tasha's scrawling handwriting. Hardly anybody left messages anymore. They either knew him well enough to call his cell phone or they left a voice mail on his office line.

These were both personal. One from Mandy, the other from Janine. They both had his cell number.

But then again, he hadn't been answering any of their calls for the past couple of weeks. He looked up when a shadow crossed in front of his desk. Tasha, an unlit cigarette hanging from her mouth, was buttoning her coat. Every morning at exactly ten o'clock, their department clerk went outside to smoke. It didn't matter how hot or how cold. "Who's the lucky one tonight?" she asked.

He shrugged.

"When in doubt," Tasha said, "use FIFO. First in, first out. Janine gets the nod. Your phone was ringing when I got here this morning. If you ask me, she's a bit needy."

He folded the slips and put them under his stapler. "I'll give them both a call later."

Tasha frowned at him. She leaned over and laid the back of her hand against his forehead. "Are you sick?"

"I'm fine. Busy." Robert yanked open a file drawer so hard that it jarred the pencil holder on his desk.

Sawyer folded his paper and frowned at him.

"Everything okay?" he asked. Then his expression changed. "Damn. Something happened at the coffee shop, didn't it?" He pushed his chair back and started to stand up.

"I handled it," Robert said, motioning for Sawyer to sit back down. "Everybody is okay, but I don't like the dad. Frank Sage is a big guy and I think he's used to intimidating people with his size."

"I've known you for a long time, Robert, and I've never seen you intimidated by anything."

Good thing Sawyer had no idea how nervous he'd been last night, when suddenly it was just him and Carmen sitting in Sawyer's living room. He'd felt as if his tongue had grown until it was too big for his mouth. Then she'd broken the tension and everything had been fine.

Better than fine. It had been one of the nicest nights that he'd spent in a long time. And he hadn't wanted it to end. When it had and he'd offered to follow her back to her apartment, he'd been afraid that she might have been offended.

She'd been on her own for a long time, successfully supporting her brother and herself. He understood feminism. Other than Sawyer, his two best other partners had been women. Both highly skilled and competent as hell.

And Carmen Jimenez was likely every bit as smart as they had been. But she didn't have the same training and she sure as heck wasn't packing a gun. A lone female, traveling at night, was a target.

It had just made sense for him to offer to follow her home. What hadn't made sense was that for the entire drive he'd debated whether he should ask to come in. In the end, he'd decided against it. Maybe it had been the memory of her running into the bathroom to avoid dancing with him. Maybe it had been that the night had been so nice that he didn't want to take the chance of spoiling it with a refusal.

Maybe it was because he hadn't figured out what to do about Carmen. He'd spent months trying to forget how she'd felt in his arms but he hadn't been able to. What the hell did that mean?

So, he'd made sure she got inside safely and he'd gone home. He'd gone to bed thinking about her, had dreamed about her, and when he'd gotten out of bed at the crack of dawn, he'd known that he was going to be waiting in that coffee shop.

Good instincts. That's what his boss had written on his last performance appraisal. Robert liked to think that he listened to his gut. And his gut had been telling him to be there.

Those instincts had been front and center when he'd pushed for the invitation to have dinner tonight with Carmen and Raoul. And he'd been happy when she'd finally said yes, insisting that she would cook.

But for some reason, he didn't feel inclined to share that information with Sawyer. "What's the plan today?" Robert asked.

"More knocking on doors. Somebody saw something."

"Maybe not. The body was found early Wednesday morning. It was below zero on Tuesday night. There probably weren't that many people out and about after midnight, not like they would have been on a summer evening."

"Well, we have to hope somebody was taking their dog out, or maybe they made an emergency run for cigarettes. We need a witness," Sawyer said.

They needed something. Right now, Robert would settle for some old-fashioned luck.

When Raoul unlocked the apartment door, he could smell the sauce. Something else, too. Something chocolate.

"Raoul," his sister greeted him. She pinched his cheek as he walked past. "How was band practice?"

"Okay," Raoul said, leaning his trombone case up against the counter. "Some girl who plays the flute had a meltdown. We had to stay late to make up the time."

"No problem. I'm running behind, too."

"Something smells good," he said. He started to reach for the brownie pan.

She stuck out her wooden spoon and tapped his hand. "You have to wait. It's for dessert."

"You never make dessert."

She shrugged. "We're having company."

They never had company. Well, almost never. Sometimes Old Lady Curtiss from down the hall ate with them. She smelled like lilacs and cough medicine.

"An acquaintance I met through work," Carmen said.

"Who?"

She turned her back to him and stirred the sauce. "His name is Robert Hanson."

A man? The only man at OCM was Jamison, his sister's boss. "What does he do there?"

"He's a police officer. A detective. You might remember him from Liz and Sawyer's wedding. He was the best man."

"Oh, yeah. He gave a funny speech at the reception."

"Yes, that's him."

"Why is a cop coming for dinner?" He walked around to the other side of the stove so that he could see her face.

"Because I asked him to. He's been helpful with a situation at work and I thought it would be nice if I fixed him dinner." She looked at her watch, then at the clock on the wall. "Shoot. I've got to get dressed. He'll be here any minute." She thrust the spoon in his hand. "Keep stirring."

She left the room as Raoul dropped the spoon in the sauce and watched it sink to the bottom.

ROBERT JUGGLED WINE, bread and a bouquet of fresh flowers as he walked up the apartment stairs. He stood outside the door and tried to remember that he'd probably gone to dinner at some woman's house at least a hundred times before.

But Carmen wasn't just some woman. She was Liz Montgomery's best friend, for one thing. She was totally hot for another. And when she smiled, it seemed as if the world suddenly became a better place.

Damn. He should take up writing greeting cards.

He'd worried that he might be late. His mother had called just as he'd walked into the florist. He'd stepped outside the small shop and stood in the cold so that he could have some privacy. It had been a short conversation. She'd apologized for bothering him, he assured her it was no bother, and then she'd dropped what might have been a zinger if he hadn't been waiting for the call for some time. *Normie is leaving.*

He'd promised to stop over the following night. That had seemed to make her happy. It was a pattern of behavior they'd perfected over the years.

He'd hung up, bought his flowers and here he was. He glanced at his watch. One minute early.

He kicked the bottom of the door with the toe of his shoe, then stepped back so that he could be seen through the peephole. He smiled and held up the loot. The door opened. A young Hispanic boy, dark and fine-boned like his sister, stood there. He was holding a fat orange cat.

"I'm Robert," he said. "You must be Raoul."

The boy didn't say yes or no. He simply stepped aside and motioned him in. "Carmen's changing her clothes."

"No problem. Where should I put this?"

Raoul pointed to the counter. The cat squirmed in his arms and he immediately bent down and placed her gently on the floor.

Robert bent down to scratch her head but she skirted away. Okay. The cat and the kid had the same sort of attitude.

Robert watched the boy walk over to the stove, immediately noting the limp, as though his right leg might be just a bit shorter than his left.

"I hear you play the trombone." Robert leaned against the counter.

"That's right," Raoul said. The kid took tongs and dug a spoon out of the sauce.

"Where do you go to school?"

"Mahoney High."

"Really? That's pretty far from here. How come you don't go to a neighborhood school?"

"Because I won't let him."

Robert whirled around. Carmen stood in the doorway. She wore a white sweater and a black skirt. It wasn't short, but tight enough to be very interesting. Her hair was piled up on top of her head in a haphazard sort of fashion.

He was struck again by how small she was. She couldn't have been more than five-three and a hundred and ten pounds soaking wet. Not his type at all.

Why was his heart pounding as if he was at the end of a 5K?

"Mahoney High School," she said, as she walked over to the stove and sniffed the sauce, "graduates more than eighty percent of the students who start there as freshman. That's almost twice as good as some of the neighborhood schools."

"Did you go there?" Robert asked, handing her the wine.

She shook her head. "No. I did the neighborhood thing."

"Looks like you turned out okay."

She shrugged. "Looks can be deceiving."

He started to make some quip about liking bad girls, but in deference to Raoul, he kept it to himself. "Should I slice the bread?" he asked.

She nodded, handed him a knife and pointed

toward a wooden cutting board on the counter. "The flowers are beautiful," she said. "Thank you."

Her tone was almost wary, and he wondered if he'd gone too far. "It's January," he said. "We should grasp on to every sign of spring we can."

She smiled. "You're right. At lunch today, Liz and I sneaked out and bought spring soap. We put some in every bathroom at OCM."

"Spring soap?" he repeated. He put the bread that he'd sliced into the basket that she passed to him.

"Yeah, you know. There are winter soaps, like cranberry-apple or peppermint-spice. Spring soaps are totally different. When you wash your hands, you can almost image that you're somewhere tropical."

"I never gave that much thought before," he said.

She laughed. "Perhaps you could buy some for the police station?"

He shook his head. "I don't think I want to be known as the spring soap guy."

"Perhaps not," she admitted. She drained the pasta and motioned for Raoul to set the table.

"I didn't know you had a cat," he said.

"Lucy is low-energy but high-strung," Carmen explained. "We got her from a shelter. She spends a lot of time hiding under the bed." She set a big bowl of spaghetti on the table. "Let's eat."

"Food's great," he said ten minutes later, meaning every word of it.

"Spaghetti is easy," Carmen said, pulling at the neckline of her sweater.

She was cute when she blushed. Robert smiled at her and then shifted his attention to Raoul. "So band keeps you pretty busy?"

"I guess."

"Your friends play instruments, too?"

"My best friend, Jacob, plays the drums."

Robert took another bite and took his time chewing. "Mahoney's got a good football team. They went to state tournaments last year."

"Yeah," Raoul said. For the first time, Robert heard the bitterness. "If you're an athlete, you've got it made."

"No special treatment for the band?"

That just got him a look. Didn't mean anything, but Robert filed the information away. "What's the gang situation like there?"

Raoul shrugged. "I'm sort of busy with my classes. I wouldn't know."

"I was just curious. I know they mix it up every once in a while in that neighborhood. I suppose drugs are a problem?"

"Not for me."

"Have you ever had anyone try to sell you something?" Carmen asked.

Raoul shook his head. "Trombone players don't get a lot of attention from the drug dealers." He stood up. "I've got a lot of homework." He carried his plate over to the sink and rinsed it.

"How are your classes going?" Carmen said.

"Fine." Raoul grabbed his backpack off the kitchen counter and walked out of the kitchen. Seconds later, a door at the back of the apartment slammed.

Carmen sat at the table and put her head in her hands. Robert scooted his chair closer. He reached a hand out and with one finger, gently stroked the back of her hand.

Carmen lifted her face. "He's lying to me. He's never done that before. Something is wrong. Very wrong." There were tears in her eyes.

"Kids lie," he said. "It doesn't mean he's in trouble. Maybe he's embarrassed about his grades and intends to bring them up."

She shook her head.

"I'll tell you what," he said. "We have cops in all the high schools. I'll talk to the ones who are at Mahoney High School. I'll see if they recognize his name. Okay?"

"Thank you," she said. "For everything."

Her face was close. Close enough that he could see the tears that still clung to her long lashes. Her skin was a lovely mocha and her lips were pink and inviting. He leaned forward. She stilled.

He bent his head and kissed her. She tasted like spaghetti sauce and red wine, sweet with just a hint of sharpness. And when she pulled back quickly, he had to force himself to let her go, to not demand more.

Her dark eyes were big.

"I hadn't planned on that," he said, proving that adult men lied, too. Maybe he hadn't exactly planned it, but for months he'd been thinking about kissing Carmen.

She didn't answer. She just looked as shaken as he felt. A few more strands of her silky hair had fallen down and her lips were trembling.

"Look," he said, "I—"

"I know you were just comforting me," she said.

He started to protest but realized that she was rationalizing the action. In her own way, she was as skittish as her cat. If she thought that he was romantically interested in her, her first instinct might be to run and hide, too. Carmen Jimenez might be twenty-nine, but he suspected she hadn't had the experiences of other twenty-nine-year-old women. She'd been too busy raising her brother.

For the first time, he felt better about what had happened at Liz and Sawyer's wedding. Maybe it hadn't been *him* that Carmen had objected to? Maybe it had just been her lack of experience and her generally shy demeanor that had sent her scurrying into the ladies' room.

This was going to require very careful handling.

If it made her happy to think the kiss had been about comfort, so be it. "Did it work?" he asked.

"I'm fine," she said. "Really, I just needed a minute."

"No problem. I'll call you tomorrow once I've talked to the cops at Raoul's school." He got up, gave her a little wave and opened the door. "Thanks again for dinner. It was great."

When he got to his car, he didn't even turn on the heat. He was plenty hot enough. One kiss and he'd been about to implode.

Very careful handling indeed.

Chapter Five

Friday

As Robert walked past Tasha's desk, she extended a long arm. Her fingernails were bright purple. "I found the name of the cop who is pulling regular duty at Mahoney High School. Horton Davis."

He took the pink message slip from her. "Thanks," Robert said. After leaving Carmen's last night, he'd left a message for Tasha, hoping that she'd work on it first thing in the morning. He pulled his cell phone off his belt.

He got the man's voice mail and he left a brief message, asking for a return call. He hoped that Raoul wasn't involved in something bad at school. He sure as hell didn't want to break that kind of news to Carmen.

Hot, hot Carmen Jimenez. Some women worked hard at being sexy. They wore the right clothes, the right makeup, had the look. He'd dated women like that and had appreciated their efforts and the end result.

But Carmen didn't seem to work at it at all. She just was.

Didn't matter if she was wearing a turtleneck and a skirt that almost reached her knees. It was the way she moved. Her natural grace. The effortless way she tossed her long, dark hair when it got in her way.

She smelled sexy.

She laughed sexy.

Damn. He was in trouble. Had known it last night when he'd gotten to his car and had sat in the cold for five minutes, letting his body temperature return to normal. After one kiss.

He fingered the pink message slips on his desk, the ones Tasha had handed him the day before. Mandy and Janine. Hell, maybe he should give one of them a call. Get things back into perspective.

He didn't pick up his phone.

Instead, he nodded at Sawyer, who was standing across the room, in conversation with Charlene Blaze.

In the morning report, there'd been the usual litany. Two gang shootings. A couple home invasions, one with injuries to the invader. Jewelry store robbery. A bank located in a grocery store had been held up. The feds were taking that one.

Just another day. More files for the desk. Especially now because, like most every detective in the city, he and Sawyer had been told to put their own cases on the back burner if possible and help Wasimole and Blaze on the serial killer case.

Their neighborhood search had turned up nothing yesterday. Nobody had seen anything. It had been cold, frustrating work, all the more so because everybody knew the clock was ticking. Another Wednesday was just around the corner. And with that came the good probability of another dead kid.

It had kept them moving even when they could no longer feel their toes and their faces were chapped from the brisk wind. They'd covered a six-block radius and had talked to countless people.

He saw that Sawyer had finished his conversation with Blaze. "What's the plan?" Robert asked when his partner approached.

"Friends and family detail," Sawyer said.

Robert had figured as much. As each of the dead boys had been discovered, Blaze and Wasimole had interviewed family and friends at great length, trying to find some thread that might tie the deceased together. But they hadn't come up with anything. Lieutenant Fischer had suggested that another team of detectives do the same, thinking that now that a few weeks had gone by for some of the distressed families, their heads might be a little clearer and they would remember something that would be helpful.

It was possible that there was nothing that connected the boys. That the serial killer was picking random victims. That certainly had been the case before. But given that the age range was so tight, the cops weren't discounting the fact that they'd missed the thread that tied all the victims together and maybe even to the killer.

"I guess we drew the short straw," Robert said.

"It's indoor work. At least mostly," Sawyer said.

Yeah, but it would be brutal, nevertheless. It was never fun talking to people who were torn up about losing their child, their nephew, their best friend. The list went on. They'd answer a few questions and then start down a tangent, recalling a special time or place that had meant something to the young victim.

He and Sawyer would listen and try to sort through the memories to try to find something that made some sense out of what seemed to be a senseless crime.

"Okay, let's get going," Robert said. "Where do you want to start?"

"Victim one. Johnnie Whitmore."

BEFORE ARRIVING AT the Whitmores' home, Robert and Sawyer reviewed the notes they had on Johnnie Whitmore. At age thirteen, he was the youngest of all the victims. Eighth-grader at Thornton Middle School. B student. Had been in Boy Scouts up until last year. Lutheran, but the family weren't regular churchgoers. On the basketball team but mostly warmed the bench. Played the clarinet. Lactose intolerant. One sister, age seven. Two-parent family. Biological mom, Michelle. Stepfather, Tom.

Their lives had been going pretty well until their son had been found by a night security guard near the entrance of a factory on Boughten Avenue.

The Whitmore family lived in a white house with green shutters. Their sidewalks were clear with snow piled two feet high on each side.

Some of that snow had fallen before Johnnie Whitmore had died. Robert wondered if the young man had shoveled the walk; maybe he'd even had a snowball fight with his younger sister.

On the porch, they could hear piano music. Sawyer cocked his head. "We had that song in our wedding," he said. "I don't know the name of it," he added. "Liz would."

Yeah, that kind of stuff was important to women. He'd dated a tax attorney the previous year and she'd spent valuable time over several years planning her wedding and documenting it on some online social networking site. Music. Dress. Everything down to the bacon-wrapped asparagus she was having for appetizers. When she'd started looking at him, sizing him up for a tux, he'd run like hell.

That was one family tradition that didn't need to be carried on.

They knocked. Michelle and Tom were expecting them. Blaze had set up the appointment the night before. Both he and Sawyer showed their badges and settled down on the leather couch in the small living room. The Whitmores sat on the love seat. There was one empty chair, a flat screen on the wall and a big, shiny piano that took up most of the far wall.

"Thank you for seeing us," Robert said. "I know that you've spoken at length to Detectives Blaze and Wasimole but given the circumstances, we wanted to have one more conversation. I know this is difficult for you."

"We want to do everything we can to catch this animal," Michelle said. She held her husband's hand.

For the next three hours, they labored over Johnnie's life, their lives. Minute details. Where was he born? Who was his doctor? Where did he go to preschool? Do you remember any of his teachers? Have you ever lived anywhere else? Did Johnnie spend time with aunts, uncles or grandparents who lived somewhere else? Where did he get his hair cut? What grocery store do you shop in? Where do you get your car fixed?

"I hope this has been helpful," Tom Whitmore said when it appeared they were finally finished.

"Yes. Thank you," Robert said. He stood up and discreetly stretched his back. "Nice piano," he said. "I saw in one of the reports that you teach lessons out of your home, Michelle."

She nodded. "I started doing that shortly after Johnnie was born. I wanted a way to be able to be at home with my kids more. Our daughter is very good for her age. Johnnie never took to it as well but at least when he started playing the clarinet, he already knew how to read music. He said that helped."

"What's that song you were playing when we arrived?" Sawyer asked.

"Beethoven's 'Ode to Joy.' I hire out for weddings. That's how I met Tom. I played at his brother's wedding. It was great extra money after I was divorced, and there's something about a wedding that just makes me happy." She licked her lips. "I need a little happiness right now," she said.

Of course she did. She'd lost her son to a maniac.

Robert and Sawyer pulled on their coats and left. Once they were back in the car, they sat there for a minute, letting the engine warm up.

"What are you thinking, Robert?" Sawyer asked.

He shrugged. "I'm thinking that I'm going to rip this guy apart when we find him."

Sawyer nodded.

"On a more practical level," Robert continued, "based on what I've seen in the other files, I didn't hear anything that rang a bell. But maybe once we talk to a few more people."

Sawyer pulled away from the curb. "First we get coffee."

TINA JOHANSON, the mother of Ben Johanson, the second boy killed, was too thin, and she chain-smoked. They met with her at her apartment right after lunch and she still had on the waitressing uniform from the overnight shift she pulled at Dill's Diner. There was no husband. Had never been a husband, according to the notes Blaze had taken. Ben was an only child. Fifteen. Freshman in high school. He qualified for free lunches.

Halfway through their questions, she pulled out her scrapbooks, slowly flipping pages, walking them through her son's short life. Robert was surprised to see the album. Most people kept their pictures on their computers and rarely printed them. But she had dutifully printed and labeled each one.

First day of kindergarten. Broken leg in second grade. Science project in fourth grade. Youth camp when he was ten. Playing the tuba in the eighth-grade band concert.

The instrument had been almost as big as the kid.

It made Robert think about the trombone case that had been propped up against Carmen's counter.

Tina had already flipped the page before Robert

held up a finger. "How long had your son played the tuba?" he asked.

"Started in sixth grade," she said, wiping away a tear. "I wanted him to play the violin but no, he insisted upon the tuba." She gave them a shaky smile. "And he was really good at it. I picked up a couple extra shifts every week so that he could take lessons from the Gottart Studio."

Robert added a line to the pages of notes he and Sawyer had already collected. *Band. Tuba. Gottart Studio.*

"I'm not familiar with the Gottart Studio," Robert said.

"On Peach Street. It's one of the best," she said proudly, as if that still brought her some satisfaction that she'd been able to provide that small luxury for her son.

They talked for another hour before finishing up. Then it was back to the cold car. Sawyer rubbed his hands together. "Her son was her life," he said.

Robert had been thinking the same thing. Now Tina Johanson was truly alone. "It's Friday," he said, stating the obvious. If something didn't break soon, they'd have another mother grieving over her son.

Robert's cell phone rang. He looked at the number and realized it was one he'd called earlier. "I need to get this," he said.

"No problem. There's a deli on the corner calling my name," Sawyer said. He got out fast, but still cold air came in and Robert turned the heater dial to the max.

"This is Robert Hanson."

"It's Horton Davis. I had a message from you, Detective."

"Yeah. Thanks for calling back. I'm working with a family who has a teenage son at Mahoney High School," Robert explained. "I wanted to see if you recognized his name. Raoul Jimenez. Dark hair, slight build. He's a freshman. No sports. Plays in the school band."

"Not ringing a bell," the man said. "But then again, there are fifteen hundred kids at this school. I can do some checking."

"Thanks. I don't want the kid to know that I'm asking about him," Robert said.

"No problem. I'll call you in a couple days," Horton Davis said.

Robert thanked the man and hung up. Then he took a deep breath and dialed Carmen.

She answered on the third ring. "This is Carmen."

"Hi. It's Robert. Robert Hanson. Are you busy?"

She seemed to hesitate. "I have a few minutes," she said finally.

"I...uh...wanted to thank you for dinner last night," he said. "It was really good."

"You're welcome," she said. She paused. "Was there something else, Detective?"

Yeah. I'd like to kiss you again. "Uh…I talked to the officer who has primary duty at Mahoney High School. He didn't recognize Raoul's name."

"Oh."

"That's a good thing," Robert said. "They know the kids who are in trouble or who *are* trouble."

"Thanks for checking," she said. She sounded disappointed, and Robert knew it wasn't because she wanted Raoul to be a known troublemaker. She just wanted some explanation for why he was pulling away.

"I wanted a chance to pay back your hospitality. How about I treat for dinner tonight?"

"Dinner?" she repeated.

Her tone suggested that she was figuring out a way to say no.

"Now, I know you're familiar with the concept. I can't promise, however, that the food will be as good as last night." He kept his tone light, which was a damn miracle of the human body, because he was literally holding his breath. "We did talk about the need to spend time together. Of course, I'd want Raoul to come, too."

There was absolute silence on the other end. He covered his phone and gulped in some air.

It was his nature to push, to force the solution he

wanted, but he backed off to give her some space. He counted to ten.

"I guess dinner would be okay," she said finally.

Robert smiled. If he always needed an enthusiastic welcome, he wouldn't have become a cop. "Good. I'll see you about seven." That would give him time to swing by his mom's house first. He hung up before Carmen could think of a reason to change her mind.

He was still staring at his phone when Sawyer opened the door. He reached out and accepted the large coffee and the plastic container. Blueberry pie. And it felt warm.

"Thanks," he said.

"News?" Sawyer said, looking at Robert's phone.

"No. It was…personal."

"I should have figured a woman. It's so cold that there are parts on my body that I'm not even sure Liz can heat and yet, you're sitting here, grinning like a fool. Mandy or Janine?" he asked, proving that Tasha didn't keep secrets well.

"Neither," Robert said, brushing off the question. "The pie looks good." He opened his container and dug in.

Sawyer stared at him, then very deliberately reached over and flipped the lid shut on the plastic container. "Damn. Please, please, tell me that you are not smiling over Carmen Jimenez. I know we all had some good pizza together and that you were helpful at the coffee shop and that she made you dinner as a thank-you. But Robert, it does not have to go beyond that. Really, it doesn't."

It was the longest spiel that he'd heard come out of Sawyer Montgomery's mouth.

And he would not lie to his friend. Was not above evading the truth, but would not lie.

"I'm taking Carmen and Raoul out to dinner tonight."

Sawyer pointed a finger in his face. "I swear to God, Robert Hanson. If you screw up and hurt Carmen and that makes Liz even just a little bit sad, you and I are taking it outside."

Robert smiled. "It's too cold outside for a Southern boy like you to want to fight. You'll get snow down your pants."

"I mean it, Robert." Sawyer leaned close. "Carmen is a very nice person."

And while his own smile didn't fade, it hurt just a little. "And I'm Jack the Ripper?"

"Of course not," Sawyer said. "Don't be ridiculous. You're my daughter's godfather. I'd trust you with her life. But I don't know if you and Carmen want the same thing."

"I think we both want to have dinner," Robert said. "It's no big deal. She's worried about Raoul."

Sawyer nodded. "Liz told me something about that. I've met him. Quiet but polite. He likes video games and one time I saw him eat about half a chocolate cake. That was after he'd wolfed down four tacos. I think he's just a normal adolescent boy."

"I agree. But Carmen is concerned. I said I'd make a few inquiries with the cop at Mahoney High. And I said that I'd try to get to know Raoul a little better. You're worrying about nothing, Sawyer. Now get your ugly hands off my pie."

Chapter Six

Raoul walked down the empty hallway, his trombone case bumping his leg with each step. Man, he'd be glad when the winter concert was over. His band teacher might just blow a gasket before that happened. Tonight, he'd actually taken a set of drums away from the kid who stood next to Jacob.

He was starving. Lunch had been seven hours earlier. Most of the time, he got some food out of the vending machines before practice started. Today, he'd been pulling his money out of his pocket when trouble had stepped around the corner.

He'd looked around but it was only him and JJ and Beau. He wasn't sure what JJ's real name was because everybody just called him JJ. He and Beau were both juniors and Raoul hated them. They'd been pretty much making his life difficult since football had ended in November and they'd suddenly had too much free time.

Beau had held out his hand and Raoul had dropped the dollar bills into it. It wasn't the first time they'd ripped him off. He'd thought about telling somebody but they'd already told him that they'd beat the crap out of him if he did that.

He believed them. They could probably bench-press his weight without breaking a sweat. He hadn't even told Jacob and he usually told Jacob everything.

It was just too embarrassing.

He'd gone to band practice hungry and been so angry that he hadn't even been able to stay with the music. He was looking forward to the brownies left from dinner the night before.

Raoul turned the corner and almost bumped into JJ and Beau. He veered to the left, hoping to get around them. Twice in one day was too much.

Beau stepped directly in front of him. "Where you going, band boy?"

Raoul didn't answer. He took a side step. "I don't have any more money," he said, hoping he sounded more confident than he felt.

"That's not band boy, that's Limpy." JJ lounged against the locker and laughed at his own joke. "That's your name, right?"

Raoul wanted to pound their stupid faces into the wall. But he knew if he tried, they'd kill him first. So he didn't say a word. He just stood there and took it.

"I saw you get dropped off for school this morning," Beau said. "Somebody told me that's your sister. She is hot, sizzling hot." He touched the gray lockers with his index finger and made a sizzling noise. "I'd like to do her."

"Shut up," Raoul said.

"Maybe we could both do her," JJ said, "at the same time."

The two of them laughed like they were the funniest things on earth. "Stay away from my sister," Raoul said.

"Oooh," Beau said, pretending to be frightened. "Like we care what you tell us to do." He grabbed Raoul's trombone case and threw it, sending it end-over-end down the hallway. It banged against the metal lockers. "Go get it."

He took a step, trying to walk around Beau. JJ stepped away from the lockers, reached out, put his hand on Raoul's shoulder and pushed down.

"Crawl."

Beau laughed. "Yeah, on your hands and knees. Like a dog. A scrawny pup from the pound."

Raoul thought about running in the other direction. But what would he tell Carmen about his trombone? She wasn't going to believe that he'd forgotten it somewhere. And if she knew these kids were hassling him, she'd be in the office, demanding that something be done.

Then it would get worse.

Raoul dropped to his knees. Then like a stupid baby, he started crawling. His backpack felt heavy and awkward and the floor hurt his knees. He could hear Beau and JJ laughing. He didn't look back until he reached his case. When he did, they were gone.

He couldn't breathe. He freakin' couldn't breathe.

He tried to stand up but he couldn't. With his back against the lockers, he slid down to the floor.

And then he started to cry.

And he hated more than he'd ever hated before.

He finally picked himself up off the floor and left the school. He got on his regular bus, rode for thirty minutes, and got off at his stop, which was three blocks from his house. He hadn't walked more than fifteen feet when the man claiming to be Hector's friend approached from behind and started walking next to him. "You're late today," the man said. It was so cold that his words came out in a puff of steam.

Raoul didn't answer. He didn't feel like talking to anybody. He walked faster.

The man kept pace. "I've got something of Hector's that he wanted you to have," he said.

That got Raoul's attention. There was nothing of Hector's at their apartment, except for a couple of pictures that had Hector in them. "What?"

"I don't want to ruin the surprise," the man said. "Give me your number and I'll text you later and let you know where you can meet me."

Raoul considered the suggestion. It wouldn't hurt

to give the man his number. If he decided he didn't want to go, he'd just ignore it. He rattled it off and the man entered it into his own cell phone.

"I still don't know your name," Raoul said.

"Apollo," he said. "Just call me Apollo. I'll be in touch."

AT TEN MINUTES after six, Robert pulled up in front of his mom's pale yellow house. It was a nice two-bedroom, two-bath Cape Cod in a neighborhood that had been predominantly Polish at one time.

She wasn't Polish. But she'd fallen in love with the house four years ago after her fifth marriage ended and she'd needed a place to live. Robert had bought it for her.

At least this time she wouldn't have to move. Norman had moved in with her.

His mom greeted him with a kiss on his cheek and pulled him into the house. It smelled like vanilla and he could see candles burning on the mantel of the fake fireplace.

"How's it going?" he asked.

"Normie has a girlfriend, someone he met at last year's Flower and Garden Show. They're moving to Florida. I'm being dumped for a longer growing season," she added.

He smiled, knowing that's what she expected. Wanted. Humor, even at her own expense, had always been his mother's fallback position.

"You going to be okay?" he asked.

"Oh, sure," she said, wiping a tear from her cheek. At sixty-seven, her face was showing the signs of age.

"What are your plans for tonight?" he asked. He hated the idea of canceling on Carmen, but he couldn't leave his mom crying at her kitchen table.

"Bingo at the church," she said. "I'm going with my friend Margie."

"You don't play bingo," he said.

She sucked in a big breath. "I do now. Margie says there's a group of retired gentlemen there, most of them widowers."

"Good Lord, Mom. Has Norman even moved his things out?"

"This afternoon. I helped him pack his truck." With the palm of her hands, she smoothed down her shirt. "At my age, you can't wait around forever. And they only play bingo twice a month."

Rebound bingo. At least he didn't have to give her the lecture about practicing safe bingo.

He stood up, pushed his chair in and kissed his mother's cheek. Ten years ago, he'd have tried to convince her that it wasn't wise to jump from the frying pan into the fire. That was two husbands ago. "Call me if you need anything," he said.

It only took him fifteen minutes to get to Carmen's apartment. At twenty minutes before seven, he parked down the block. He left his car running, knowing that the temperature inside would drop in minutes if he killed the engine.

He closed his eyes and tried to block out the last half hour. It didn't work.

He had a bad gene pool. Maybe Sawyer was right to be worried about Carmen. What was it that he'd said? *Not sure Carmen and you want the same thing.*

What did he want from Carmen?

He wanted to kiss her again. That was a given. He'd managed to keep from blurting that out, thankfully.

He wanted more, though. To hear her laugh. And watch her move around her kitchen in a tight black skirt with a towel tossed over one shoulder. To see her eyes, content with pride, when she watched her brother shovel in his spaghetti.

None of that spelled danger for Ms. Jimenez. Sawyer was worried about nothing.

Robert checked his watch and decided to wait another five minutes. He didn't want to appear overanxious, yet he wanted to be prompt.

That was respectful.

Sawyer would be proud.

At seven minutes before seven, Robert pulled into a parking space in front of Carmen's building. He opened the main door of the three-story building and walked up the stairs to the second floor.

Then, as he had the night before, he knocked on the door.

Carmen opened it. She wore a high-necked, long-sleeved cream-colored sweater and matching slacks. She'd left her dark hair down and it fell over her shoulders to midback.

She looked fabulous.

And she smelled even better. Something spicy that hinted that there was more to Carmen than met the eye.

Or was that wishful thinking on his part?

"Hi," he said. "You look nice."

She blushed. "I wasn't sure where we'd be going."

"Maxine's."

She frowned. "That's expensive, isn't it?"

He waved a hand. "They're running a winter special," he said. "Where's Raoul?"

"In his room. I'll get him. Excuse me," she said.

Robert stood near the door. He could see the cat. She was scrunched under the couch, watching him. "I'm not here to steal the silverware, Lucy," he said, trying to sound friendly.

No response from the cat.

He could hear the murmur of voices from the back room. They went on. And on. And he was just about to barge down the hall and fix whatever needed to be fixed when Carmen appeared.

"Raoul is sick," she said. "He thinks it's something he ate for lunch."

Okay. Plan B. "No problem. We can order in," Robert said.

The words were no more out of his mouth when Raoul appeared behind his sister. He was dressed in jeans and a sweatshirt and his hair was sticking straight up on his head.

"I told you, sis. I want you to go. I'm not three. I can take care of myself. You deserve to have a nice dinner."

Robert could see the indecision in Carmen's eyes. He kept his mouth shut. He didn't want to take the chance of reminding her that the dinner invitation had been about the three of them bonding.

"You're sure?" Carmen asked.

Raoul rolled his eyes.

"I'll bring you back some chicken noodle soup," she said.

"Fine." He turned and went back into his room.

Robert worked hard to keep the smile off his face. "He probably just wants to get some sleep."

Carmen grabbed her bright blue cape from the closet. She stuffed her hands into dark gloves. "I know that I need to treat him more like an adult. It makes him crazy when I baby him. It's just that I've been taking care of him forever," she said, her voice quiet.

"You have been. And you've done a great job. If you don't mind me asking, what's the story behind Raoul's leg?"

"He's had it from birth. It's actually a problem with his hip but it looks as if his legs are not the same."

"Doesn't look as if it slows him down much." Robert wrapped an arm loosely around her shoulder. "Give him some space. It'll be fine."

They had barely pulled away from Carmen's apartment building when she dug her feet in. "If we go to Maxine's, I want to pay my half."

Robert counted to ten. "That's not necessary."

"Yes, I insist. I wouldn't be comfortable any other way."

Well, hell. She'd been right earlier. Maxine's could get a little pricey. There was no way that he was imposing that kind of expense on her budget. He had some idea of what social-worker types made and he doubted there was much left at the end of the month.

"Maybe we could go somewhere else?" he suggested.

"Gordon's is close. I love their soup."

He made a quick right. Gordon's had been a neighborhood favorite for years. It had a tile floor, worn booths, surly waitresses and great comfort food. Sometimes he and Sawyer had lunch there.

It wouldn't break anybody's budget. "Whatever floats your boat," Robert said easily. He found a seat as far away from the door as possible, knowing that every time the door opened, cold air would blow in. They read the plastic-covered menu, and then he ordered the meat loaf special, and Carmen got a turkey club with broccoli soup.

There was a young couple in the corner with a squealing baby. An old couple was in the next booth, both reading sections of the newspaper. A young black man, wearing a white apron that came to his knees, was unloading clean glasses and cups onto the shelves.

He'd never brought a woman to Gordon's before. Never even considered it. The women he dated were generally successful in their own careers, had discretionary spending and expected him to have the same.

Both Mandy and Janine would have been severely disappointed in Gordon's.

"What's so funny?" she asked.

He hadn't realized that he was smiling. "Nothing," he said. "Just thinking that Sawyer will be jealous. He loves the hot beef sandwiches here."

She glanced around. "I imagine it's not your usual place for dinner."

There was an underlying message in her simple words. It went sort of like this. *I realize you had something different in mind, but this place is really more me, which is just one more sign of how different we are.*

She wasn't the only one who had studied human behavior in college.

"I think I'm ready for the unusual," he said.

Her dark eyes widened. But at that moment, the waitress returned, slapped their food down and refilled their water glasses. Carmen picked up her turkey sandwich and chewed. She looked very thoughtful.

Robert dug into his meat loaf. It was delicious. And the potatoes were equally good. Neither of them spoke for several minutes. Finally, she pushed her plate away. She'd eaten her soup and most of her sandwich.

"I should be getting back," she said.

He nodded and motioned for the waitress. He ordered a large chicken noodle soup to go. Carmen unzipped her purse and started pulling out money.

"Please," he said. "It's on me. Consider it payback for the spaghetti, although I certainly got the better end of the deal."

She hesitated and then nodded. She leaned back against the booth and yawned.

"Tough day?" he asked.

"Sort of. Uncooperative pregnant teens can be a bit trying on the nerves."

"How are things with Alexa Sage?"

"Okay. I got a message from her today. In the presence of her father, she told her mom the news. I guess there were lots of tears but it sounds as if everybody held it together."

He felt a chill run down the back of his neck.

Which was crazy because the air from outside was blowing in his face. "Don't let your guard down around that man. There's something about him that I really didn't like."

"I won't. But I'm hopeful that he'll get past his disappointment in his daughter and give her the support she needs."

"I don't think his daughter was too confident of that and she knows him best, right?"

"Yes, but teenagers don't have the reasoning skills to understand that adults, once they've had time to assimilate new information, have the capability to deal with all kinds of things. When a kid messes up, she can't imagine that her parent will ever be able to understand why she did it or how she could have made such a mistake."

Her eyes were serious and her voice soft. There was pain in both and he wasn't sure what had put it there. "But I bet you're good at painting the picture that things can get better," he said, wanting to make her smile again.

It must have worked. She lifted her water glass. "Here's to sharp crayons," she said. And she took a big drink. "How was your day?"

"Cold," he said. "Irritating because we're not making more progress on the case. Plus," he added, "I had to go see my mother. Her husband is leaving her." He wasn't sure why he told her. He never talked about his mother.

"Oh, no," Carmen said.

He waved a hand. "It's okay. I mean, she's sad and all. But she's been through this before. Sometimes she's even the leaver, not the leavee."

She was looking at him as if he had two heads.

"I know that sounds bad. But she's been married six times and she's had a couple live-ins, as well."

"I see," said Carmen.

There was no way. Nobody could understand it.

"She likes being with someone, being part of a pair," Carmen said.

That was a nice way to put it. "Yeah, well, she's the left shoe and she enjoys the search for the right shoe very much, but then she quickly tires of wearing the same pair so she has to go shoe shopping again."

She smiled. "I bet she's fun."

He nodded. "She is and she's my mom so I can't stay irritated with her for very long."

"Of course not," Carmen said.

Five minutes later, they got in the cold car and he drove to her apartment. "It will probably be hard to find parking," she said. "You can just drop me off."

He smiled and kept driving. She wasn't getting rid of him that easily.

As they neared the building, she put her hand on the door handle. It looked as if she was ready to make a break for it.

"I'll walk you in," he said. "I want to make sure Raoul's doing okay," he added.

He found a parking spot, pulled in and was around the car before she could get her seat belt undone. They walked up the stairs to her apartment and she unlocked her door.

When she opened the door to the apartment, he saw that almost every light in the apartment was on. They hadn't been when they'd left. That was a good sign that Raoul had been up and about, so maybe the kid was feeling better.

"I'm going to check him," she said.

He watched her walk down the short hallway, appreciating the view. Her slacks weren't tight but just snug enough to hint at a nicely rounded bottom.

He heard the door open and then slam shut. When Carmen returned to the living room, her face was pale and her eyes were big. Robert's protective instincts shot up a notch.

"What's wrong?" he asked, already moving closer.

Chapter Seven

"He's gone," she said. "He's not in his bedroom."

"Check the other rooms," Robert instructed.

It didn't take her long. There was only her room and the bathroom. She came back into the hallway and shook her head.

"Does he have a cell phone?" Robert asked.

Carmen nodded.

"Okay, check your cell phone for messages and then try his phone," he said. "I'm going to take a look at his room."

He supposed it was a typical teenage boy's room. It looked a little bit like he remembered his own room. Posters on the walls. Dirty clothes in the corner. A single bed with covers in disarray.

There were no signs of a struggle.

No hastily prepared note propped up against the pencil container. No clue as to why a sick fifteen-year-old boy would suddenly be gone.

He looked up. Carmen stood in the bedroom

doorway, cell phone in hand. "Nothing. And he's not answering. It went straight to voice mail."

"Does he ever do this? Go out without letting you know?"

Carmen shook her head. "No. I mean, he goes out on his own, of course. But not usually at night. Not without telling me. And he was sick. Oh, my God, maybe he had to call an ambulance." She stopped. "No, that's ridiculous. He would call me before he'd call an ambulance."

Robert could see when the full realization of the situation hit Carmen. Raoul hadn't called her. So either something had prevented that or he simply hadn't tried.

There was no sign of struggle, and the door had been locked.

"It's possible he was lying," she said. "Maybe he wanted to get me out of the apartment and figured he'd have a couple hours of free time. He thought we were going to Maxine's."

He appreciated that she wasn't going to refuse to consider alternate realities. Her work with teenagers had taught her that teenagers lied.

"He had on jeans and a gray sweatshirt earlier. Do you see them anywhere?" Robert asked, sweeping his hand around the room.

Carmen shook her head. "His coat is a red jacket with a hood. I don't see it, either."

"Okay. We'll assume that's what he has on. I'll call it in. Get our guys watching for him."

She reached out a hand, stopping him. "Robert," she said, her voice subdued. "I don't know what he's up to. I want to hope it's not something bad. And I know that I don't have any right to ask you to look the other way. But—" her voice cracked "—I don't want him to be arrested. When that happened to Hector, things got so much worse. It was the beginning of the end."

He hoped like hell Raoul hadn't done something stupid that was going to make this woman sad. He was going to really have to kick his butt. He put two fingers under her chin and tilted her head up. "Here's what I think," he said. "Raoul is a good kid. I don't think he's involved in anything that's going to get him arrested. Stop worrying. We're going to find him. Now, why don't you start with his friends?"

He watched while she scrolled through the numbers in her phone. He believed everything he had said to Carmen. The kid was probably fine. But just in case, he called in Raoul's description to dispatch. He felt immediately better after doing that. It wouldn't hurt for a whole lot of eyes to be looking. He sent a text to Sawyer, letting him know. Within seconds, Carmen's phone rang.

She grabbed for it. "Liz," she said, looking at him.

Robert nodded. "I figured it wouldn't take long."

Carmen answered and the women talked for a few minutes. While he couldn't hear Liz's side of the conversation, she evidently was volunteering to come over because Carmen repeatedly assured her it wasn't necessary, that she should stay home with her baby. Carmen ended the conversation by assuring her friend that she'd call her if anything changed.

A half hour later, nothing had changed and they didn't know anything more. Robert and Carmen had both tried his cell phone multiple times.

Carmen had talked to some kid named Jacob twice. She'd explained that he was Raoul's best friend and that they often carpooled in the morning. After school, they each took different buses because Jacob's house was a couple miles from their apartment. After the first call to Jacob and learning that the boy hadn't talked to or seen Raoul since band practice had ended, she'd waited while he also tried to reach Raoul. She'd called a second time only to learn that Raoul wasn't answering any of Jacob's texts or calls, either.

Carmen sat at the table, her shoulders bowed, her head in her hands. Robert pulled his chair close and put an arm loosely around her shoulders. She seemed even smaller than usual, as if she were deflated.

He was so going to kick the kid's butt if he was out fooling around and making his sister worry needlessly. If it was something more serious, he hoped he had the wherewithal to help Carmen deal with it.

He wanted to be out on the street, looking for Raoul. But he knew that he couldn't leave Carmen.

So he simply sat with his arm around her. Maybe they'd sat for ten minutes when they heard footsteps on the stairs. Carmen's head sprang up.

"Relax," Robert whispered.

They heard the key in the lock and the door opened. Raoul, wearing his red jacket, his gray sweatshirt and his blue jeans, walked in. He was carrying a bag from Walgreens.

"Hi," he said. He looked surprised to see them.

Carmen ran to him and hugged him tight. He tried to duck her embrace. "What's going on?" he asked.

"Where have you been?" she asked. She held his face in her hands. "I've been worried sick. You didn't answer your phone. I called you at least ten times."

Raoul pulled his cell phone out of his pocket. "It's dead," he said. "I was going to charge it when I got home."

"You said you were sick. Too sick to go to dinner with us."

"I started to feel better. I remembered I needed some things for school. I'm sorry, Carmen. I didn't mean to worry you."

"Don't ever do that again," she said, her tone gentle. "I mean it. For goodness' sake, we had the police looking for you."

That got Robert a swift and unfriendly look. Which Robert might have been inclined to ignore if his gut wasn't telling him that something was very wrong. The kid had looked like death warmed over an hour ago. Yet minutes ago, his steps on the stairs had been quick and light. His color was good.

Maybe it was possible that within minutes of their departure, he'd suddenly felt much better and had remembered the school supplies. But it was Friday night. There was no school tomorrow. He'd have had the whole weekend to buy school supplies.

Maybe he needed them for a project he had to complete this weekend?

Or, maybe, as Carmen suggested, he'd heard Maxine's, figured that his sister would be out of his hair for at least two hours and took off, fully expecting to be back before she was any the wiser.

He'd pulled similar stunts when he was Raoul's age.

And rarely gotten caught. His mom had been busy wooing the next potential husband, and that had left little time to watch over a busy and sometimes rebellious teen.

"You need to get some sleep," Carmen said. "I'll see you in the morning."

Raoul mumbled good-night as he walked past

Robert. Very quietly, Robert took a deep breath. He waited until he heard Raoul's bedroom door shut. "He smells like grilled onions," he said.

Carmen frowned. "I guess."

Robert shrugged. "I don't want to make too big a deal out of it but the kid didn't want anything besides chicken noodle soup to eat an hour ago. Now he smells like he swam in a vat of cooked onions, like maybe he got one of those steak sandwiches from the guy on the corner two blocks down."

Carmen chewed on her pretty lip. "I'm just grateful that he's okay," she said finally. "Thank you," she added. "For being here. For being a voice of reason. For knowing what to do. I swear my brain just stopped working."

"I still want to do dinner with the two of you. Maybe tomorrow."

She shook her head sharply. "Tomorrow. No. That's impossible."

Robert had learned years ago that sometimes retreat was an essential component of an effective offense. "No problem. I'll give you a call," he said. He gathered up his coat and gloves. "Take care," he said.

And he left without touching her.

RAOUL HEARD THE apartment door shut and pulled his sack out from underneath his bed. His hands were still shaking. He'd seen Carmen and that cop sitting at the table and thought for sure that they would want to see what was in the bag.

He opened the thin plastic and pulled out the heavy black gun. He pointed it at the Spider-Man poster on the wall. *Bang. Bang. Take that, super-hero.*

Apollo had sent him a text about ten minutes before his sister knocked on the door to tell him that Robert was there. He'd already agreed to go to dinner and he had to do some fast talking to get out of it so that he could meet Apollo. But he'd been really anxious to see what Apollo had of Hector's.

He'd sure as heck never expected that it would be a gun. Raoul ran his hand across the barrel and could almost feel his brother in the room with him.

Carmen didn't like guns. Didn't even like it when Raoul played video games where there were guns.

She never had to know.

But just having it made him feel better. Made him feel closer to Hector. Made him feel like he wouldn't always be the kid who got pushed around.

He put the gun and the box of bullets that Apollo had given him in his backpack, underneath his history book.

Chapter Eight

Saturday

At ten the next morning, Robert was impatiently standing in line at a coffee shop. Sawyer usually took coffee duty, but they'd split up this morning. Sawyer was running down the Gottart Studio and Robert was following up on red handkerchiefs. They had identified three more retailers that carried the product. That was in addition to the four large retailers that they'd already spoken to.

Unfortunately, these three stores were small shops and they didn't have information systems that tracked all their sales data and could spit out reports at the push of a button. The big stores had been able to tell them the day and time the product had been sold. Had even been able to tell them if the merchandise had been purchased with a credit card or cash. Unfortunately, all the red handkerchiefs purchased in the last six months had been bought with cash.

The three places this morning hadn't even been able to tell him that. And they had no recall of any specific customer who had purchased one or more of the handkerchiefs, which generally came in packages of three.

It made Robert sick to think of how many packages their guy might have bought.

He shuffled forward and gave his coffee order to the sixteen-year-old girl at the counter. She'd just given him his change when his cell phone rang. "Hanson," he answered.

"Horton Davis here," the caller said. "I had a chance to check out Raoul Jimenez late yesterday afternoon and figured you might be anxious to hear. He's a freshman. Plays in the band, just like you said. Quiet kid. Small for his age. No known gang affiliations. That's about all I can tell you."

"That's enough," Robert said. "I appreciate it."

"No problem. Wish this school had fifteen hundred just like him." The man hung up.

Robert waited about fifteen seconds before dialing Carmen's cell phone. There was no answer. He scanned the numbers in his phone until he found Options for Caring Mothers. He remembered adding it last summer when Sawyer had been fixated on Mary Thorton and her pretty counselor, Liz Mayfield.

He figured it was a good idea to call the office. Carmen seemed the conscientious type who might work a few hours on a Saturday morning even if she didn't have to.

The phone was answered on the third ring.

"Carmen Jimenez, please," he said.

"I'm sorry, but Carmen isn't in today. Can I take a message?"

Not in. Holy hell. She wasn't doing something stupid like meeting Frank Sage and his daughter again, was she? "Is she out of the office on business?" he asked.

The receptionist didn't answer. "May I take a message, sir?" she asked again.

"Can I talk to Liz Montgomery?" he said.

"Just a moment, please," she said.

Liz picked up within seconds. "This is Liz Montgomery."

"Hey, Liz, it's Robert." He heard the quick inhale of breath and knew that she'd immediately jumped to the worst possible conclusion. "Sawyer is fine. This call is not about him," he said quickly.

There was a shaky laugh. "Sorry," she said. "What can I do for you, Robert?"

"I tried Carmen and she's not in. Do you know where she is?"

Liz sighed. "Robert, you are my husband's best friend and I think the world of you. I know you were at Carmen's last night and I'm really grateful that she wasn't alone, waiting for Raoul to come home. But Carmen is like a sister to me. I just have to ask. What's going on here?"

He adored Liz but he'd been a cop way too long to put all his cards on the table. "Carmen asked me to check with the officer at Mahoney High School to see if he knew anything about Raoul. I heard from him this morning and wanted to pass on the message. She didn't answer her cell phone."

"You just want to pass on a message? That's it?"

"Yes, ma'am."

Liz sighed, loudly. "I swear, what is it about cops? Haven't you heard that transparency is the new thing? And don't you 'Yes, ma'am' me. That's what Sawyer does just before he convinces me to get up, put my feet on the cold floor and fetch him coffee in the mornings. But if you must know, I did expect Carmen for a couple hours this morning but she called in sick. I'm sure she's at home sleeping and didn't hear her phone."

"Thanks, Liz. Appreciate it."

He tried Carmen's cell one more time, and again there was no answer. He grabbed his coffee from the counter where it had been sitting for a couple minutes and was out of the building in less than thirty seconds.

Ten minutes later, Robert knocked on Carmen's door and stepped back so that he could be seen through the peephole. He heard a noise on the other side. He waited but no one opened the door.

He knocked again. "Hey, Carmen, it's Robert. I called your work and they said you were at home."

No answer, but he heard a quiet sniff and he got nervous. "Carmen. Either open the door or I'm going to break it down. Your choice."

No answer.

"Okay. Stand back because I'm going to shoot your door lock off."

Because he was watching the peephole, he saw the quick flash of dark, proof that she'd looked out. She must believe him. Robert rubbed the bridge of his nose, where a full-blown, knock-you-on-your-butt headache was started to brew.

She opened the door a crack. "I'm busy," she said.

He could see the middle six inches of her face and body. "What's wrong?" he asked.

"Nothing's wrong."

"I don't think that's true," he said in a very conversational tone. "I can only see a little bit of you but your nose is red and your voice sounds like you've either been on an all-night smoking binge or you've been crying. I'm guessing crying. Did something else happen with Raoul?"

He heard her sigh. "I don't want to talk about it."

"I talked to the cop at Mahoney High School," he said.

There was no response. "What did he say?" she asked finally.

"Open the door and I'll tell you." He'd learned to play dirty in preschool.

Slowly, the door opened. She had on old jeans, a sweatshirt and absolutely no makeup. Her eyes and nose were both red and she had a box of tissues in one hand.

"What did he say?" she asked again.

"Just tell me one thing," he said. "Are either you or Raoul hurt, sick or in danger?"

She shook her head. He smiled at her and wrapped an arm around her shoulder. He pulled her toward the couch. "Good. Then whatever else is wrong, we'll fix it."

She tried to pull out of his embrace. He let her go but when he sat down, he grabbed her hand and pulled her down next to him. When she immediately scooted several inches farther away, he smiled at her again. Smart woman. Having their thighs touch was probably not a good idea. Especially if they intended to have any conversation.

"Want to tell me about it?" he asked.

She shook her head.

Okay. That stung. He had this overwhelming urge to comfort her, to make it all better. "I'm a really good listener," he said. "They teach you how in cop school."

That got him his first smile. As absurd as it sounded, he thought the room lit up a bit. That even the plants in the window glowed a little greener.

"I can't," she said. "My issue. My problem. What did your contact say? Did he find out anything about Raoul?"

Robert looked down the hallway. "Is he sleeping still?"

Carmen shook her head. "Music lessons and then his friend Jacob is having a birthday party. He won't be home until late afternoon."

"Okay. Well, the cop at the school figured out who he was and basically doesn't think you've got anything to worry about. He's not a troublemaker and he's not running with any gang. I'm guessing his problem is that he's fifteen. Nothing worse than that."

"I hope you're right," she said, not sounding convinced. "But thank you for checking. I really do appreciate it."

"Okay. Show me," he said.

Her eyes widened.

He stood up. "I need somebody to share my popcorn with at the movies. You've got your choice between a Gerard Butler action movie, a Keanu Reeves action movie, or a Matt Damon—"

"Let me guess," she interrupted. "Action movie."

"How did you know?"

She laughed. "Just lucky."

He felt the first easing of the pressure on his heart. He didn't want this woman to cry. Ever again.

"But I'm sorry," she said. "I just can't."

"Philosophically opposed to cinematic entertainment?"

She shook her head. "No. That's a ridiculous question. But my reasons don't really matter. You can't go anyway. I've read the paper. Every cop is working overtime on this case."

"True. I'm working all day tomorrow. But I do get a couple hours of R & R today. You like ice cream, right?"

She frowned at him, not following his abrupt change of topic. "Of course, but what does that have to do with it?"

"Near the movie theater is the best ice cream shop in all of Chicago."

"It's freezing outside."

Robert smiled. "The lines will be shorter."

Carmen took a deep breath and looked around her apartment. Finally, her gaze settled on him. "I need some time to shower."

"No problem. I'll just sit here and wait. I've got my phone, which means I've got my emails, and I'll work on those while you're getting ready."

"You've got an answer for everything, don't you?"

She was giving him way too much credit. He felt as if he were on a train and it had run off the tracks. He was hurtling through time and space.

All he knew was that he wanted an afternoon with Carmen, with no worries about work or Raoul or anything else to cloud the horizon. He held up his phone. "If I don't have the answer, I'll just search for one on Google."

She shook her head. "I'll be ready in forty-five minutes. And I need to be home by six."

CARMEN COULDN'T REMEMBER ever having more fun at the movies. Of course, she hadn't been to the movies with a man in a very long time. The last time someone had paid for her ticket, it had been four dollars. She'd been almost embarrassed when Robert plunked down a twenty for the two of them and hadn't gotten any change back.

They walked up to the snack counter. She pulled money out of her pocket and after a quick glare, he let her pay for the treats. They each got a soda and a large popcorn to share. Robert picked out a bag of M&M'S candy. He raised one eyebrow at her and when she nodded, he dumped the whole package into the popcorn.

"Now we have to get married," he said.

She shook her head at him. "I never marry on the first date."

"Okay. We can probably go out a couple more times before we tie the knot."

He looked so serious. She could feel her heart

rate accelerate. She thought she might pass out until he winked at her.

She started to feel a little dizzy again, however, halfway through the movie, when Robert reached over and gently held her hand, his thumb caressing the soft inner flesh of her palm. She knew it meant nothing to him. But when she closed her eyes, she could shut away the world, shut away her memories, shut away the knowledge that thirteen years ago to the day, something had happened that had changed her whole life. His warm hand, his soft touch, it all gave her a little bit of peace.

They left the theater shortly after four, her hand still in his, and walked along the frozen lakefront. The weather was the warmest it had been in days, maybe weeks, and the wind was almost nonexistent. The sun wasn't as warm as it had been at noon but still it had to be at least thirty degrees.

"It feels almost tropical," she said. "That is, if one wears a hat, scarf and mittens in the tropics."

He looked around. "Seems like a spring soap kind of day."

She nodded. "Yes. Very mangoish."

"Mangoish?" he repeated. "Is that a word?"

"It is in the spring soap world." But he was right. It was as if someone had opened the cage and let all the mice out to play. Old people in pairs, young women in knee-high boots and moms pushing baby strollers that probably had a baby in them but all you could see was blankets.

She turned away from the strollers, not willing to let them intrude on her happiness.

"Ready for the ice cream?" Robert asked.

"I guess. I'm going to need to get home soon. I like to be there when Raoul comes home."

"He's having cake. That's means you've got time for a double chocolate chip in a waffle cone."

"Okay. But one scoop."

He took her to an old-fashioned ice cream shop with white tables and red chairs. It was at least half-full, proving that it was never too cold for ice cream. Of course, the owners had the place toasty warm, making it easy to forget that winter raged outside.

She ordered a single scoop of butter pecan in a cup, and he got the waffle cone with two scoops of chocolate chip. He found them a booth in the corner, and they took their coats off. A young girl wearing a short red skirt, a white ruffled blouse and a red hat brought the ice cream to the table.

Halfway through her ice cream, Carmen sighed. "This is so good. Raoul is going to be mad when I tell him that I had homemade ice cream. He loves desserts."

"Based on the meal I had at your place, I think the kid is eating pretty good most nights. I dreamed about those brownies and I woke up craving caramel and chocolate."

She waved a hand. "They're easy," she said, dismissing the compliment. But it left her feeling warm inside.

"Where did you learn to cook?"

"From my grandmother. She lived with my family. There was always a pot simmering on the stove and something baking in the oven. I'm sure she'd think I was a terribly lazy cook." Carmen mockingly glanced over both shoulders. "Don't tell anyone," she said, her voice soft, "but I buy my refried beans in a can. No soaking and boiling for me."

He smiled. "No problem. I buy mine already spread on a burrito shell and topped with melted cheese. And they get passed through the drive-through window."

She shook her head in mock disgust. "They should not call that Mexican food."

"Maybe not, but the city has some great Mexican places. I'll take you to my favorite spot for enchiladas."

She swallowed hard, feeling as if she had a pecan stuck in her throat. He'd said it so casually, as if it was a foregone conclusion that they'd be seeing more of each other.

As if they were going to start dating.

Which was preposterous. Yeah, maybe she had told Liz that she'd consider the online thing. Raoul was getting older. Maybe she could start dating. But she needed to start with someone who was equally green at the game—maybe some nerdy guy who lived at home with his mother and collected comic books.

Like one of the guys from *The Big Bang Theory*.

She certainly wasn't going to start with Robert Hanson.

She quickly finished her ice cream and pushed the empty dish aside. "I should be getting back," she said.

Robert nodded and helped her with her coat. Once outside, she saw that the streetlights were on and darkness was fast approaching. "Do you want to catch a cab?" Robert asked.

She shook her head. This was her favorite time of day to be out. It still felt safe and the city was always prettier when the lights were on. "It's only seven blocks," she said. "Let's walk."

Two blocks down on the corner, a travel agency had big posters of tropical locales in their front window. She stopped to take a better look. "Speaking of tropical," she said, "doesn't that look wonderful? This time of year I'm envious when anyone talks about their warm-weather vacations."

"Aruba, Bermuda or the Cayman Islands?" he asked, letting his eyes run down the alphabetized list of destinations. "What's your pleasure?"

She smiled. "All of them. One right after another."

He reached for the door handle. "Let's see what they've got."

He was serious. Oh, good Lord. "I was only kidding," she said, pulling his hand off the door handle.

He looked her in the eye. "Too late. I can see the way to your heart is hot sand and an icy rum drink."

The way to her heart? He was teasing, but it made her feel warm all over to think that he was looking for a path. Robert Hanson was a very nice guy, and she really couldn't remember ever having a better day.

"I really have to be getting home," she said.

"Okay. We'll put this conversation on hold for now."

When they got to the front steps of her building, it suddenly seemed awkward. She still didn't know why Robert Hanson had knocked on her door or why he'd spent the afternoon with her.

"Thanks for the movie," she said.

"My pleasure."

"And the ice cream, too."

He nodded. "Likewise. The popcorn and M&M'S were great."

Too bad they hadn't had time for more food. Their conversation could have lasted through the night. She climbed up two of the steps. "I guess I better go."

"Can I ask you something?" Robert asked. He looked serious.

No. "Sure."

"Can I call you?" he asked.

So he hadn't missed that she'd been evasive back at the ice cream store. He'd evidently decided on a more direct approach. Well, maybe she should follow suit. "Why? Something tells me that you're not the type to spend your time going to movies and eating ice cream."

He considered. "I think you're wrong. I had a great time this afternoon."

He sounded as if he meant it. "Maybe," she said, letting him know she wasn't convinced. "I guess you could call me."

He nodded. "Good. You know we're going to talk about why you were crying," he said, so casually that she almost missed it.

"Not today," she said.

He nodded. "Okay, not today. Maybe not even tomorrow or the next day. But soon. I don't want you to be upset. When you are, I want to know why."

"You can't fix everything, you know?"

He shrugged. "Who says?"

She rolled her eyes. "I have to go." She took a step and her cell phone rang. She pulled it out of her purse and looked at the number. *Alexa Sage.*

"Hi, Alexa, this is Carmen." She listened, interrupting just once. "Slow down, Alexa. You're hard to understand."

After a minute, she nodded. "Okay. I'll meet you at the coffee shop in twenty minutes. Pack an extra outfit in your backpack and we'll worry about the rest later. It's going to be okay, honey."

She put her phone back in her purse and met Robert's eyes. "Alexa and her dad had a big fight. She's leaving home. I'm going to meet her and have her stay with me tonight until I can find her a place tomorrow."

Chapter Nine

"Is she hurt?" Robert asked, already pulling out his own phone.

"No. He didn't touch her or her mother. Just a lot of yelling and slamming doors and threatening to kick her and her pregnant belly out into the cold."

"She's a minor child. We can call child welfare services."

"We could but they aren't going to do anything. They've got a backlog of cases involving really young children that are going to be higher in the pecking order. The best thing to do is simply get her out of there."

She was probably right. "Don't you think having her stay here is a little bit like waving a red flag in front of Frank Sage? He's already not crazy about you and suddenly you're harboring his wayward daughter."

Carmen shrugged. "I'm not going to have her stay in a hotel by herself, and I'll need at least a day to work out housing in one of our group homes. It will be fine. It's just for tonight, maybe two nights at the most. But I really need to get going if I'm going to be on time to the coffee shop. I wish Raoul was here. I'd feel better if I knew that he was home safe."

"I'll stay and wait for him," Robert said. That way he'd be there when Carmen and Alexa returned. Just in case dear old Dad decided to follow her. "What's his friend Jacob's number just in case I need to track him down?"

Carmen scrolled through her phone and rattled it off. Robert entered it into his own phone.

Robert used Carmen's keys to let himself into the apartment. It seemed longer than five hours since they'd left. The movie had been good. Sitting in the dark, holding hands with Carmen, sharing popcorn laced with chocolate, had been pretty damn fabulous.

That stupid crack about having to get married had just popped out of his mouth. Had no idea where it had come from. Certainly after hearing about the litany of husbands his mother had collected, she'd understand why he wasn't the marrying kind.

He hadn't wanted the afternoon to end. But he could only stretch out a bowl of ice cream for so long. On the walk back to her apartment, he'd found himself thinking about whether she might invite him in and then wondering what he would do if she did.

As though he were a seventeen-year-old boy on a date with the head cheerleader.

Thank God Sawyer wasn't around to witness how pathetic he was. Speaking of which, he should check in. He'd left a message for his partner earlier when Carmen had been in the shower.

"Hi, it's me," Robert said. "Got a minute?"

"Not much more than that," Sawyer said. "It's my turn to cook and I'm making jambalaya. The rice is almost done."

Robert smiled. The image of Sawyer, one of the toughest cops he'd ever worked with, sitting home waiting for rice to boil, was pretty damn amusing. "Were you able to check out the Gottart Studio?"

"Yeah. Good call on your part. Ben Johanson and Henry Wright both took music lessons there."

Victims two and four. "But not the other boys?"

"Not on the customer list. I called Michelle Whitmore just to make sure that Johnnie hadn't taken lessons there and she'd never heard of the place."

That was disappointing. "So we've got one slim link between two of the kids. I guess that's more than we had before."

"Absolutely," Sawyer said. "You can chase it down tomorrow, although I do think a whole lot of middle-school kids play an instrument."

"Yeah, I think it gets them out of a science class or something like that."

"Maybe," Sawyer said. "Got to go. I don't want my rice getting sticky."

RAOUL WAITED IN line for the diving board, his arms wrapped around his naked chest. He didn't like swim parties. He was always the skinniest kid there. Even so, when Mrs. Minelli had called and invited him to Jacob's surprise party, he hadn't been able to say no. After all, Mrs. Minelli cried easily. She used to cry at soccer games and everything. And Jacob was his best friend.

But Jacob was mad at him. Mrs. Minelli didn't know that. Probably not many knew it besides Jacob and Raoul. Carmen couldn't know it. She'd freak out. She'd start asking a bunch of questions and he'd have to lie to her.

It had been a mistake to show Jacob the gun. He'd gotten all freaked out, said that Raoul was going to get arrested. Had gotten so loud that Raoul had needed to tell him to shut up. Jacob had told him that he was going to laugh when Raoul needed bail money. Had told Raoul that he was crazy to take a gun from somebody that he didn't know just because the guy claimed to be a friend of his brother's.

But Jacob never had a brother who'd died. Jacob maybe didn't understand everything.

Now Jacob came up and stood behind him in line. He didn't say a word. Two more people jumped off the board. They moved up. Raoul had his foot on the first step of the ladder.

"I don't know why you came," Jacob whispered.

Raoul didn't turn around.

"I don't know why you want to spend time with a bunch of kids when you could be out shooting people."

Raoul whipped around. "I already told you once. Shut up."

"Hey, maybe you can join a gang, too. That would be cool. Who wears blue?" Jacob pointed at Raoul's swim trunks.

"You don't know what you're talking about," Raoul said.

"You're so stupid," Jacob said. "I'm not even going to feel bad when they find you all shot up."

Raoul could tell his friend was about to cry. "Jacob, look—"

"Hey, you're holding up the line," someone yelled from the back.

Raoul climbed up the remaining eight steps. He turned one last time to his friend. But Jacob was gone. Raoul looked around and saw Jacob and Pete, another kid from class, jump into the shallow end. They were laughing.

Screw it. Screw them. He didn't need any of them. He jumped off the board, not bothering to kick to the surface until his lungs were about to explode. He swam over to the side, picked up his towel and walked over to Mrs. Minelli.

"I'm not feeling so good," Raoul said. "I think I better call my sister."

"I'm sorry to hear that." Mrs. Minelli grabbed his chin and gave him a close look. "Did you eat too much before you swam?"

"Yes, that must have been it," Raoul said.

"You boys," Mrs. Minelli scolded.

"Well, I guess I'll go get dressed."

"Jacob will be so disappointed."

Jacob wouldn't even know Raoul had left. If he did, he sure wouldn't care.

Raoul thought about calling Carmen to pick him up. She was expecting him to get a ride home from Mrs. Minelli. It didn't matter. It was warm enough to walk home.

He'd been walking for less than a minute when an old black car pulled up. The passenger door swung open. Apollo was driving. There was an open beer in the cup holder next to him.

"Hey, Raoul. Want a lift?"

Carmen would kill him if he got in a car with somebody who had been drinking. "No, thanks," he said. "What are you doing here?"

"Last night you mentioned that you had a birthday party here today."

He had. Apollo had asked him if he wanted to

learn to shoot the gun on Saturday and he'd had to tell him why he couldn't. But he hadn't expected the guy would be hanging out, waiting for him. What if Carmen had picked him up? What if she somehow found out that he had a gun in his backpack?

"Look, I've got to get home," Raoul said.

"How's your sister?" Apollo asked.

"She's okay, I guess," Raoul said, feeling uncomfortable with the question.

Cars were swerving around Apollo's car and some were honking their horns.

"Get in. We can talk some more."

Raoul slid into the car. The car smelled bad, sort of like the locker room but different. "Does Carmen know you?"

Apollo shook his head. "We met a couple times when Hector was alive. But that was a long time ago. So, do you have the gun?"

Raoul nodded and pointed at his backpack. "It's heavy."

"Yeah. Meet me tomorrow night at ten o'clock and I'll show you how to shoot it."

Ten o'clock. Carmen would never let him leave the apartment at ten o'clock on a Sunday night. "I don't know," he said, not willing to admit that he might not be able to get out of the apartment.

"Speedy's Used Cars. Don't disappoint me, Raoul." Apollo pulled up next to the curb and motioned for Raoul to get out. Once he did, the black car sped away.

Ten minutes later, Raoul was a half a block from his apartment when Beau and JJ came around the corner. They didn't look surprised to see him. What the hell were they doing in his neighborhood? He had no idea where they lived, but he doubted that it was nearby. He'd been living in the area his whole life and he'd never seen them around before.

"Hey there, Raoul," Beau said. "All done with your little friend's birthday party? Did you play pin the tail on the donkey? Oh, never mind. It was at a pool. It would have been pin the tail on the porpoise."

"What are you doing here?" he asked. He felt braver than usual. Maybe it was the gun in his backpack. "How did you know about Jacob's party?"

"Aren't you full of questions?" JJ said.

"I help out in the office," Beau said. "'Cause I'm such a good kid," he said mockingly. "Your friend's mother came in and was telling one of the office bitches all about it. I looked up your address. Thought it might be nice if we knew where you lived."

"Why?"

He shrugged. "Haven't you heard, Raoul? Knowledge is power. We own you. You better bring more money to school next week for lunches."

They walked past him. Beau bumped into his shoulder, sending him sideways. They never looked back.

He walked the rest of the way home, feeling sick to his stomach. He unlocked the door and pushed it open with his foot. Once inside, he stopped. The cop was sitting at his kitchen table.

Could the day get any worse?

"What are you doing here?" Raoul asked.

"Hi. Nice to see you, too." Robert took a drink of coffee that he'd evidently helped himself to. "Your sister had to go help a client. She should be back soon."

"So now I need a babysitter?"

Robert shrugged. "Carmen didn't want you coming home to an empty apartment. She cares, Raoul. That's not really something to be mad about."

"Whatever." He bent down to pick up Lucy, who had suddenly appeared from wherever it was that she'd been hiding. Raoul gently slung her over one shoulder. "I've got things to do in my room."

"No problem," Robert said, as if he couldn't care less what Raoul did. "How was the birthday party?"

Man, was Carmen telling this guy everything? "Fine," he said. He opened his bedroom door, went inside, and slammed it shut behind him.

ROBERT DRUMMED HIS fingers on the table, more agitated than he'd been in some time. It had been a crazy day. Some deep lows. Some big highs. Like Carmen licking her butter pecan ice cream off her spoon—that vision was likely to keep him up a few nights.

And then the call from Alexa. Big downward dip. Not that he didn't appreciate and understand Carmen's commitment to OCM's clients. After all, he was pretty committed to his work, too.

But why the hell did this particular commitment have to involve Frank Sage? Robert had gotten a look at the guy's eyes. They were so angry.

Plus for the past half hour, he'd been wondering just what it could have been that had made Carmen so sad. Sad enough that she'd been crying hard.

Was she worried about money? He'd give her some.

Had someone been mean to her? He could make that stop fast.

Was it simply the stress of trying to raise a fifteen-year-old on her own?

Wasn't sure how to make that better. He'd been a fifteen-year-old boy at one time but he sure as hell didn't know anything about parenting one.

He heard the downstairs door open and then footsteps. Quiet voices. Carmen came in first. She was smiling, and he took that as a good sign.

"Hi," she said. "Raoul get home?"

"Yes. In his room."

She turned to the young girl behind her. "Alexa, you remember Robert Hanson?"

The girl nodded. "I think my dad does, too."

Good. That's the way he wanted it. Robert stood up. "Does your dad know that you're here?"

"I don't know. I told my mom. Not sure if she'll tell him. I don't think he cares," she said.

Robert wasn't so sure. "What's next?" he asked, looking from Carmen to Alexa.

"Alexa will stay here tonight, and then tomorrow we'll visit a couple places where she might stay for the duration of her pregnancy and for a few weeks after delivery."

Well, it sounded as if they had a plan. And it didn't include him.

That was okay. He had his own plans for tomorrow. Another Wednesday loomed. He'd be solo tomorrow. Sawyer had worked his extra shift today because Liz's parents were celebrating their fortieth anniversary and Sawyer and Liz had a command performance for lunch in the suburbs.

Sawyer had said that he might be back in time to join the rest of the department as they helped Wasimole turn fifty on Sunday evening at Bolder's, his favorite neighborhood bar. There'd be beer, darts, pizza and stupid humor.

Just what Robert needed to get his head back on straight. To keep him from thinking about raising teenagers and consoling crying women.

There'd been some discussion about canceling the party but in the end, Lieutenant Fischer had settled that. He was smart enough to realize that what the group needed was a couple hours to blow off steam before they hit it hard again.

Robert put on his coat and buttoned it. "I'll check in with you on Monday." *Check in.* That was lame but it was the best he could come up with.

"Thank you, again," Carmen said. "For today. For waiting for Raoul. For everything." She stepped forward and brushed her lips across his cheek.

He felt his heart flip in his chest. Didn't think it was medically possible but was pretty sure that was what had happened.

"No problem," he lied as he walked out the door.

He had a very big problem.

Carmen Jimenez was getting to him. Big-time.

Chapter Ten

Sunday

Robert was in the office by seven the next morning. He spent a few hours tackling the paperwork that seemed to multiply overnight. He wasn't the only one working, and somebody had tossed a box of doughnuts on the break-room table so the morning wasn't a total loss.

At ten, he dialed the number in Gabe Monroe's file. Victim number three. The only African American in the group. The rest of the kids had been white. Gabe was fourteen and a freshman at Liekert Academy, a charter school that had opened less than ten years earlier. Mom worked in retail and his dad for the park district. Had a much older brother in his third year of a football scholarship at Notre Dame. Had a sister who was just a year older.

The phone rang. No answer.

He waited ten minutes and tried again. Same result.

He looked up the address. It was less than twenty

minutes away. And Carmen's apartment was on the way.

Fifteen minutes later, he was knocking on Carmen's door. She opened the door a foot and peeked around the edge. All he could see was her head and part of her shoulder. Her silky hair was floating around her face and her skin was bare, with the exception of the narrow straps of her very little blue tank top.

"Hi," she said. "Shhhhh." She put a finger to her lips. She smiled self-consciously. "I know it's almost eleven but Raoul and Alexa are still sleeping. Teenagers," she said, shaking her head.

"Did I wake you?" he asked.

She shook her head. "I've been up for hours. Already drank a pot of coffee. Very quietly. Alexa was wired last night. We watched movies until the wee hours of the morning. I think she was trying to avoid thinking about the real world for a while."

"I just wanted to make sure everything was okay," he said.

She smiled and stepped out into the hallway, almost closing the door behind her. She was wearing blue-and-white-plaid flannel pajama pants that rode low on her hips and the little shirt. He could see a line of bare skin where the pajama pants stopped and the shirt didn't start.

Holy hell. He could feel his body get hot.

"I wanted to thank you again for yesterday," she

said. "I'm not comfortable saying much more than this but I want you to know that I'm very grateful for what you did. The movie. The ice cream. It was really just what I needed."

He nodded. More gratitude. It was nice but not what he was interested in. He edged forward just a little, feeling off balance. His coat felt too tight and the muscles in his legs were jumping.

He couldn't move. All he could do was stare, like some adolescent boy at his first girlie magazine.

Her breasts were fuller than he'd imagined and he could see the outline of her nipples. Her waist and hips were slim but so feminine. And her skin was a beautiful mocha color.

"You're beautiful," he said.

Her eyes widened and he knew that he'd surprised her.

Well, hell, this was going to shock her, then.

He reached for her and pulled her into his arms. Then he angled his lips over hers and kissed her.

For the briefest of seconds, she was still.

Then she opened her mouth and welcomed his tongue. He felt the jolt, the sharp shock, all the way to his toes.

He kissed her for several long minutes, learning her mouth, nibbling on the corner of her lips. Then, very slowly, he slid one hand underneath her shirt, running his hand up her ribs. When she didn't resist, he angled his hand so that his thumb brushed over her bare breast.

She groaned, and he pulled her in tighter to his body. He regretted his big coat but focused on the feel of her hot skin against his hand. He breathed in, taking in her scent, holding it deep in his lungs.

He shifted his hand, just slightly, to cup the full weight of her breast. He lifted the edge of her shirt, desperately needing to taste her.

She moaned and sagged in his arms. He thought his own knees might give out. He bunched the soft material of her shirt into his hand and raised it, exposing one small, round, beautiful breast.

He bent his head and licked her nipple.

She shook in his arms.

He closed his mouth and sucked her gently.

And a door down the hallway opened.

Robert moved fast, pulling the shirt down, shifting so that Carmen was protected from prying eyes.

The old woman, a big purse on her arm, shuffled by. "Morning, Carmen," she said, amusement in her tone.

"Morning, Mrs. Curtiss," Carmen answered, her voice muffled by his coat. "Have a nice day," she added, her voice fading at the end.

"Oh, you, too, dear," the woman said. She walked down the steps, leaving a trail of lilac in the air.

Carmen didn't move until the downstairs door

opened and closed. Then she couldn't get out of his arms fast enough.

Her cheeks were pink and her lips, her gorgeous lips, were trembling. She put a hand to her forehead. "It's a good thing she has a strong heart."

It wasn't what he'd expected, but then Carmen Jimenez was a constant surprise. He ran a hand across his own jaw. His own heart was still pumping pretty fast. "It's likely she's seen people kiss before."

She gave him a look that probably made pregnant teenage girls sit up straighter in their chairs. "I think we were a little past that," she said.

Yeah. But not nearly far enough. "Look, Carmen, the circumstances might not have been perfect but—"

She held up her hand. "Please. I don't want to talk about this. Not right now. I have to go," she said, edging back toward the apartment door.

"But—"

She shook her head, stepped inside and softly closed the door.

He knew that he was fast enough that he could get it open again before she locked it. He could force his way into the apartment, force her to talk to him.

But he didn't do anything like that. He just took his trembling legs and his tingling fingers back out into the cold.

WHEN ROBERT RANG the doorbell at the Monroe house, he knew somebody was home because he could hear the television right through the walls of the small Cape Cod. This was a section of the city where the houses had all been built in the forties and fifties, mostly of brick, and close together. Garages were all detached and people got to them through the alley that ran behind their houses.

Nobody came to the door. Robert bypassed the bell, took his fist and pounded on the wooden frame. He got someone's attention because the television got turned down and he could hear locks turning on the door. An old African American woman, wearing a bright orange housecoat and no socks, opened the door.

Robert held out his badge. "My name is Detective Robert Hanson, with the Chicago Police. I wanted to talk to Maurice or Carol Monroe."

"Maury and Carol aren't here," the woman said. "I'm Maury's mother. It was my turn to watch the dog."

Robert didn't see or hear any dog.

"Tippy's asleep," the woman said. "She doesn't hear so well anymore."

Right. The television had probably damaged her ears. "When will they be back?"

"Tuesday night."

They could have another dead kid by the following morning. "Would you have a few minutes that I could ask you some questions?"

She waved him into the house. The furniture was leather, the hardwood floor gleamed with polish and the television was a newer flat screen. There was a fat bulldog sleeping in one of the chairs.

"I'm sorry about the death of your grandson," Robert said.

The woman nodded. "Gabe was a good boy. His death has been hard on my son and his wife. His brother, too, of course. But probably the hardest on his sister, Trina. Being so close in age and everything, they've been best friends since they were babies. I told Maury and Carol that they better get her away from all this for a few days. Especially after that last boy got killed."

"I was wondering if Gabe played any musical instruments."

She shook her head, and Robert could hardly contain the disappointment he felt. He'd been so sure that this was the thread that tied the murders together and that somehow, someway, he'd be able to figure it out.

"You're sure?" he asked.

"I'm his grandmother. I think I would know. His sister played the drums for a few years but Gabe was always more interested in soccer."

Robert stood up. "I'm sorry to have bothered you."

"Did all the other boys that died play an instrument?" she asked, proving that she was sharper than he'd given her credit for.

"Yes, ma'am, they did."

"Well, I'm sorry I couldn't be more help. I want you to find this person who is doing all these awful things to these boys. I want you to find them and I hope they resist arrest and you blow their brains out."

She said it calmly, as if she were commenting on the price of lettuce at the store.

"We'll do our best, ma'am." Robert closed the door behind him and went back to his cold car.

JUDY FRANCONI WRIGHT answered the door with a glass of red wine in her hand. The family resemblance to Alderman Franconi was evident, although her features were more feminine, of course. She seemed more relaxed than her brother, who was always wound tight.

Maybe it was the wine.

Hell, if he'd lost a child, he might just stay drunk.

"Mrs. Wright?" he said. "I'm Detective Robert Hanson."

She motioned him in. "Detective Blaze said that you'd be stopping by. My husband isn't here. It's difficult for him, I guess."

He heard the bitterness and was pretty confident that he got the underlying message. *It was difficult for her, too, but she was stepping up, handling it.*

"No problem. I know that you've provided a great deal of information to Detectives Blaze and Wasimole but I have a few more questions."

"Can I get you a glass of wine before we start, Detective?"

"No, ma'am. Maybe a glass of water?"

"Of course." She left the room and returned within minutes with his glass. She'd refilled her own wineglass.

"My son, Henry, was a remarkable young man," she began.

And Robert let her talk. And when he got the chance, he asked all the questions on his list. When it was over, he felt confident that he'd gotten the information he needed, and Judy Franconi Wright seemed almost happy that she'd gotten to talk about her son, that she'd gotten the opportunity to share significant moments of his life, even if it was with a stranger tasked with investigating the details of his death.

Toward the end, he circled back to the Gottart Studio. While they had been able to connect only two of the dead boys to the place, Robert couldn't shake the feeling that there was something more there.

"You mentioned that Henry played the cornet in his middle school band."

"First chair," she said proudly.

"And I understand that he took music lessons at the Gottart Studio."

"For years. The cornet isn't his first instrument. He also plays piano and drums. You know, just a couple weeks before he died, someone from the Stalwart Academy contacted him. They were trying to recruit him. One of their representatives had met with him several times."

While he hadn't ever heard of the Gottart Studio, he had certainly heard of the Academy. It was a private high school for the arts. Both of Lieutenant Fischer's kids went there. He occasionally bitched about the tuition but Robert had always gotten the impression that he was really happy with the education and the opportunities. Lots of their graduates got full scholarships to good colleges.

Robert made a note. *Stalwart Academy. Recruitment.* He looked up. "What was the representative's name?"

She wrinkled her brow in concentration, then shook her head. "I'm sorry but I never got his name." She paused. "I guess I figured there'd be plenty of time for that." She picked up the wineglass that she'd set aside while she reminisced and took a big drink.

Robert stood up and put on his coat. He handed her his card. "If you think of anything else that might be helpful, don't hesitate to contact me. Anytime."

ON SUNDAY NIGHT, at ten minutes after ten, Raoul waited in the shadows near the front entrance of Speedy's Used Cars and prayed that he wouldn't throw up. He tilted his head to the right, then the left, trying to stretch his neck. He switched his gun from his right hand to his left and wiped his sweaty right palm across his black jeans. How the hell could his hand be sweating when it was freezing outside?

An hour ago, he'd gone to bed, making a big deal that he was really tired. And then when Carmen and Alexa were in the kitchen, he'd slipped out the front door.

But now he'd been outside for at least forty-five minutes. All the time thinking about Carmen and how disappointed she'd be. He had to make sure she never found out.

"Let's go, my friend."

Raoul jumped a stupid foot. His heart pumped so fast he thought he might be having one of those heart attack things that Jacob's mother was always worrying about.

"Did I scare you?" Apollo wrapped an arm around Raoul's shoulder.

"No," Raoul lied, stepping out of the man's grasp.

Apollo laughed. "Let's go. We're going to accomplish two things tonight. You'll get some target practice, and Speedy will learn not to sell cars that stop running in three weeks."

He held out his hand. "Let me see the gun."

Raoul handed it to him, and his heart stopped again when Apollo pointed it at him.

"Bang," the man said, laughing. He turned away from Raoul. "Now here's how you hold it. Use two hands. And when you press the trigger, it's going to give you some kickback. Don't fall on your butt and embarrass yourself."

Raoul did what Apollo told him to do. He liked the feel of the gun in his hand. It made him feel powerful.

"Now, here's what you need to do. Get around that fence and aim at the windshields. Speedy's going to be sweeping up glass for weeks. Now, go."

Raoul slipped out of the shadows and ran toward the chain-link fence. At one end, between the fence and the building, there was just enough space for a skinny kid like him to squeeze through. He stood in the middle of the dark lot and pointed his gun at the first car. He squeezed the trigger and heard the sound of breaking glass. Dang. It felt like his shoulder popped out of place. He swung his body to the left, more prepared this time. Another pump

on the trigger. More glass. Three times more he repeated the routine.

Dogs started barking. Raoul took one quick look
over his shoulder. Across the street, lights flashed
on in two different houses. He started to run toward the fence. Just as he went through, he heard
the sounds of a siren.

He jerked, ramming his chest into the jagged
wire. His coat got caught. He pulled, heard the
material rip, and then he was free. He grabbed at
the piece of material that was stuck in the wire and
then ran the opposite direction of the siren, zigzag-
ging through a backyard and around a Dumpster
in the alley.

He ran down the dark alley, his arms pumping
at his sides, his breath coming in big gulps. He
heard a noise and looked behind him. Headlights,
harsh and bright, bore down on him. Raoul leaped
to the side, his body crashing into the brick wall.
The car screeched to a halt next to him. The front
door swung open and Apollo sat inside, laughing.

Raoul wanted to lift his gun one more time.

"Get in, my friend."

In the distance Raoul heard the sounds of more
sirens. He jumped into the car.

"Good job," Apollo said. "You did good."

"I've got to go home," Raoul said.

"Don't worry, my friend. Cops are stupid."

Raoul didn't say anything. It took ten minutes

for the car to pull up outside of Raoul's apartment building. Raoul got out, feeling every pound of the gun as he hoisted his backpack over his shoulder.

Chapter Eleven

Monday

"Hanson, wake up."

Robert lifted his head from his desk. He had either malaria, West Nile virus or the worst hangover of his entire life.

"Go away." He peered at Tasha through very sore eyes.

"Exactly how many shots did you do with the birthday boy? You know Wasimole drinks like a fish."

"The next time he turns fifty, I'm not going to help him celebrate." Robert leaned back in his chair and barely avoided moaning. The room literally spun.

"Get going. Report begins in three minutes."

Robert managed to drag his poor body into the crowded room. It was quieter than usual, no doubt because at least half the department had been at the party. It gave him little comfort that several looked worse than he did.

Robert sank down onto a chair. He hadn't had a hangover for years. Now he remembered why. They made you feel like hell. Not that he didn't like to tip one or two. He knew how to party. A little booze, some cards, a pretty woman. His life. It was a damn good one, too.

All those things had been available last night. But after he'd drunk too much and lost thirty bucks in poker, he'd gone home alone. Not for lack of trying on Tara's part. He'd dated her once or twice before. Nice girl. Wasn't exactly sure how she'd ended up at the party last night but thought he remembered that she was friends with one of the new female recruits who had gotten hired last year.

Tara had been playing dirty last night, rubbing up against him, making sure he knew she was interested in more than the cards in his hand.

It just wouldn't work. He couldn't go home with Tara. Not when all he could think about was Carmen Jimenez. About how her lips tasted, sweeter than any ice cream. About how her skin smelled. About how her eyes looked, shimmering with tears.

So he'd kept drinking until Tara had gotten tired of waiting and moved on.

Now, as he sat up straighter as Lieutenant Fischer walked to the lectern, he'd pay a price for that. He tried to keep his eyes from glazing over as the lieutenant went through the events of the previous twenty-four hours. Two rapes. One murder. Five domestic calls, two to the same residence. Burglary. Assault and battery. Vandalism.

He almost missed it. Speedy's Used Cars. He knew the place. Not much and not in a great neighborhood. He wouldn't normally think twice about it. However, the firsthand witness accounts of a young, thin, dark-haired boy with a slight limp running from the scene had his head clear in about three seconds.

There had to be a lot of kids who matched that description. Robert didn't care. He only knew one. Raoul Jimenez.

And the way Sawyer was looking at him, he was thinking the same thing. Robert shrugged. Sawyer knew him well enough to know that he'd check it out.

Kids make mistakes. Robert kept reminding himself of that, all the way out of the department, to his car and on the way to Raoul's school.

He parked in the teacher's lot. He went to the office, showed them his ID and asked for Raoul. They gave him a room to wait in and within five minutes, Raoul stood before him, looking confused and scared.

"Sit down." Robert motioned to the chair next to him.

"I don't want to sit down. I want to know what's going on. Has something happened to Carmen?"

It made it more difficult to kick the kid's butt

when he so clearly cared about his sister. "This is not about your sister. It's about you. I'm here as a police officer," Robert said.

Raoul dropped down onto the chair. "Okay."

Robert gave him his best hard-ass cop look. "Do you want to tell me what you were doing last night?"

Raoul stood up and started pacing around the small room. "Sleeping."

"No, you weren't."

"Who says?"

"A couple eyewitnesses who live across from Speedy's Used Cars."

"I don't even know where that is."

The kid had evidently rehearsed his lines. "Really?"

Raoul nodded.

"I don't believe you."

"I don't care."

He was keeping up the tough-guy act pretty well. It reminded Robert of many of the conversations he'd had with the *boarders* in his mother's house. "Okay. That's good enough for now. But if I find out differently, you're going to regret ever having lied to me."

"The only thing I regret is that my sister and I had dinner with you."

"Trust me on this. It won't be the last time."

"Are you going to be freakin' spying on me?"

"No. I lo…like your sister." Whoa, had he almost said *love?* Maybe he had really enjoyed kissing her and holding her and he'd been able to think of little else than how she'd looked in her pajama pants and little shirt. Or how she'd tasted when he'd taken her in his mouth.

But love?

Raoul stared at him, like he'd suddenly grown a third eye. It seemed appropriate since he felt as if his head was going to explode.

"Don't you have to read me my rights or something?" Raoul asked.

Robert shook his head and took a deep breath. "You've watched too many episodes of *Law & Order.*" He leaned toward the boy. "Look, Raoul. I'm worried about you."

Now Raoul studied the ceiling. "I've got to get back to class. We're having a social studies test."

Robert nodded. "Okay. But watch yourself, Raoul. 'Cause I'm kind of like a bad penny. You just never know where I'm going to turn up."

He left the building and dialed his cell phone on the way to his car. His mom answered on the third ring.

"Hi. How was the bingo?" he asked.

"Pretty good," she said. "Even distribution of men and women. At my age, you don't see that all that often. You know, men are the weaker species and they die off sooner."

"You doing okay?" he asked.

"Oh, sure, honey. Don't worry about me."

"I'll try to stop by later this week," he said.

"I'm free on Thursday," she said.

There might be another dead kid by then. Robert sucked in a breath of cold air. "See you then."

He was halfway back to meet Sawyer when his cell phone rang. It was Sawyer. "Ten minutes," Robert said.

"That's not why I'm calling. I just talked to Liz. She said that Carmen called in, said she'd be late, that somebody had vandalized her car. I made sure a squad went out to get the report but I thought you'd want to know."

Damn straight. Robert did a fast U-turn in the middle of the street, ignoring the horns that blared in response. He was at Carmen's apartment in less than ten minutes. She was standing outside, wrapped in her blue cape. A beat cop he didn't recognize, with his coat collar pulled tight to protect against the cold, stood next to her. He'd parked his squad car in front of her damaged car.

Robert parked and got out. He flashed his badge at the beat cop.

"Officer David Smith," the young man said in response, extending his hand.

Carmen didn't seem as happy to see him. She was frowning at him. "How did you know?" she asked. Then she waved her hand. "Never mind. I just figured it out."

Robert looked the car over. The driver's side had a streak of white paint, starting at the front fender and running down the length of the car. The passenger-side window had a hole in it, as if someone had taken the end of a baseball bat and poked it through.

It was damage that could have been done without anyone even getting out of their car. Which made it unlikely that there would be any physical evidence at the scene.

"Any ideas?" he asked Carmen.

She shook her head. "No. Not even sure when it happened. I parked the car about eight last night. I'd planned to start work later today since I've got evening appointments tonight. I came out around nine and saw this."

"Where's Alexa?"

"She and Raoul left for school around the same time. Raoul wanted me to take him to school but it was Mrs. Minelli's turn to drive. Alexa took the bus. They must not have seen this or they would have come back inside and told me." She paused. "You look tired," she added.

"I'm okay," he said.

She nibbled on her lower lip. "Late night?" she asked, her voice lower.

Robert glanced at Officer Smith, who was looking down at his report but no doubt listening to every word. "Birthday party for one of my coworkers."

She waved a gloved hand. "It's none of my business."

Maybe not, but they sure as hell had unfinished business between the two of them. If the old lady who lived down the hall hadn't come along, who knows where that business might have taken them. "I went home alone," he said very quietly.

Her cheeks seemed to get a little pinker. "Why?" she whispered, locking eyes with him.

Because I can't think about anybody but you. She wasn't ready for that kind of admission. He decided to play it safe. "I'd worked all day. I was tired."

"Of course."

It was twenty degrees outside but the air suddenly seemed warm, maybe even a little oppressive.

Smith stepped forward. "I'll get you a copy of this report for your insurance company," he said. "At least you can still drive it."

Neither Robert nor Carmen said anything. After several seconds, Carmen spoke up. "Thank you for coming so promptly," she said.

The young officer looked from Carmen to Robert and offered up just a little smile. "No problem." If he'd wondered initially why a detective was showing up at the scene of a car vandalism call, he wasn't wondering anymore.

Robert waited until the man was back in his car. Then he shook his head to clear it. He needed to get back in the game. He took a step away from Carmen, trying to get away from her scent, something that evoked visions of good brandy and silk sheets. "Sage?" he asked.

She shrugged. "I have no reason to think that."

"Who else is pissed off at you?"

She rolled her pretty brown eyes. "Maybe it was just random violence. Maybe," she said, evidently warming up to the topic, "it was somebody who was angry that I had a parking space. You know how nutty people in Chicago get when it snows."

She was right about that. Street parking was always limited in the city, but when piled-up snow took up several spots, it became somewhat of an Olympic sport to protect one's parking place. People dragged furniture out of their homes to block their neighbors from taking an empty spot. Just last week, in one of the more affluent neighborhoods on the north side, there'd been a hell of a fight when a woman had used her Lexus to push a couch out of the way.

It was possible that Carmen was right. Robert looked up and down the street. Many spaces were open because people were already at work. But for the cars that remained, there was no similar damage. He shook his head. "I don't think so. No other cars were touched. Face it, Carmen. Somebody went after your vehicle. This is personal."

Robert knew where Frank Sage lived. He'd made it a point to look it up that very first day, after the coffee shop incident. Now he drove there, knowing that Carmen would probably be upset if she knew what he was doing.

He didn't expect Sage to be there but based on what Carmen had said, it was likely that Mrs. Sage would be home. And right now, he wanted the woman's perspective on her husband's state of mind.

He knocked on the screen door of the modest home. The place had white siding and red shutters, and looked to be a two-bedroom or maybe a small three-bedroom. He saw the curtain move on the interior door.

He held out his badge. "My name is Detective Robert Hanson with the Chicago Police. I'd like to talk to you about your daughter."

Well, sort of. Whatever it took to get the door opened.

Mrs. Sage opened the door halfway. She looked briefly at his badge. "Is my daughter okay?"

"Yes. As far as I know. May I come in?" he asked.

She opened the door the whole way in response and turned her back. She walked over to the couch, picked up the remote, and turned off the television. Then she sat.

It was a small room, maybe twelve by fourteen, and one end was open to the kitchen. The appliances were dated and there were ugly placemats on the table.

The only chair in the living room was a worn recliner, and Robert figured that was where Frank Sage settled in every night. Not wanting to sit there and also not wanting to tower over Mrs. Sage, he walked over to the kitchen table and grabbed one of the wooden chairs. He brought it back into the living room and sat.

"Thank you for seeing me," he said. "Did you happen to tell your husband that Alexa is staying with Carmen Jimenez?"

She nodded. "When she didn't come home on Saturday night, he wanted to know where she was."

"It was my understanding that he threatened to kick her out. That there was quite a scene here before she left."

She nodded again. "You have to understand. My husband, well, he says things that he's sorry for later on." She pushed her short brown hair behind one ear, then did it again when the strand wouldn't stay back. "He's a good man. He just works too hard."

Why did she feel that she needed to defend the

bully? "Alexa said that he hit you after you dented your car."

Her face lost its color. "She shouldn't have said anything. That's our business."

"You know," Robert said, softening his voice. "There are places that can help you. Places you can go."

The woman said nothing.

Robert felt sick. While Mrs. Sage didn't resemble his mother physically, they were very much the same person. Afraid to be alone. Ready to settle. Too quick to forgive or forget.

Too willing to accept that they had no value without a man.

He wasn't going to be able to convince her, any more than he'd been able to convince his mother. "You're going to have a grandchild," he said, giving it one last try. "Your daughter needs your help."

Again the woman said nothing.

Robert stood up. "Carmen Jimenez's car was vandalized last night or early this morning. I'm going to go see your husband at his work. If I have any reason to believe he's involved, I'm going to arrest him. If I have any reason to believe that he's going to hurt Alexa or Carmen, I'm going to make sure he doesn't have the chance."

Mrs. Sage walked over to the door and opened it. Robert put the chair back where it belonged and walked out. He was halfway down the sidewalk when Mrs. Sage spoke.

"Tell Alexa that I love her," she said. Then she closed the door.

Chapter Twelve

Frank Sage worked at a factory that was fifteen minutes from his house. On the way there, Robert passed the coffee shop where Carmen had met Alexa that morning. Sage had been nearly out of control that day. Robert had hoped he might settle down, but if he wasn't going to, then Robert was just going to settle his ass down for him.

When he got to the factory, they refused to let him see Sage until he showed them his badge. Then they got significantly more cooperative and stuffed him in a small conference room with a round table and four chairs.

Robert didn't sit.

When Sage came in, he didn't, either.

"What the hell are you doing here?" Sage asked, taking the offensive.

Robert rubbed his chin. "I told you I'd be watching you."

Sage didn't answer. He just crossed his arms over his broad chest.

Robert decided to get to it because he was fast losing the battle with his inner self, who wanted to beat the crap out of Sage's smug face. "I want to know where you were between the hours of eight last night and nine this morning."

"I was home the whole night. Watched the nine o'clock news and then I went to bed. My wife can verify that."

Great.

"I got up this morning, stopped for coffee on my way to work at my usual place, and got here at twenty minutes before seven. I punched in and I've been working ever since. My supervisor could verify that. He's a jerk who watches his employees like a hawk. He'd know if I was gone."

Supervisor was probably hoping the guy would make a break for it. "That should be easy enough to verify and trust me, I will."

Sage shrugged. "Why the questions?"

"Carmen Jimenez's car was vandalized either late last night or early this morning."

Sage's face showed no reaction. "I don't care. About her, her car, her anything. She's nothing."

Robert forced himself to breathe deep. "I want you to know that if I find out that you had anything to do with it, I will arrest you so fast that your head will be spinning. Stay away from her and stay away from your daughter."

"I don't have a daughter," Sage said. He opened up the door and left the room.

Before Robert left, he did exactly what he'd promised Sage. He asked the receptionist to get the supervisor.

He was a young guy, maybe thirty. He had a pencil stuck behind one ear and he was carrying his phone in his hand. His name was Hank Riser.

"What can I do for you, Detective?" he asked.

"Mr. Riser, I'm investigating some vandalism that occurred either late last night or early this morning. I'm trying to verify what time Frank Sage arrived at work this morning and whether he's been at work the entire time."

The man pushed a button on his phone. "Frank is usually in before me but I can check his time-card punch." He used his index finger to scroll through a couple screens. "Yes, he was here when his shift began at seven and I saw him probably a half hour later. He's been here all morning." The man looked up from his phone. "What's this about, Detective?"

"Just trying to put some pieces together," Robert said. "What your general impression of Frank Sage?"

"Stays mostly to himself at work. Gets here on time. Leaves the minute he can."

"You ever have any trouble with him getting along with others?"

The man took a deep breath. "Not that's documented. But I've had a couple of the women in the shop tell me that they aren't comfortable working next to him. It's nothing he says or does, it's just a feeling they get. So I move them to another area and we get past it."

It's just a feeling they get. He understood that. Maybe they wanted to push Sage's face into a brick wall, too.

Robert shook the man's hand. "Thank you for your time."

He walked back to his car and kicked his tire for the hell of it. He didn't have enough evidence to bring Sage in.

He got in, started the vehicle, and texted Sawyer. On my way back. Be there in fifteen.

He was five minutes away from his destination when he saw the jewelry store. He'd shopped there a few times over the years. A necklace here. Some earrings there. They did a nice job with wrapping birthday and Christmas gifts.

There was an empty parking spot in front of the store.

He took that as a sign.

"Can I help you, sir?" the young woman behind the counter asked.

"Yes," he said. "Yes, you can."

WHEN ROBERT SAT down at his desk, Sawyer looked up.

"I expected you forty-five minutes ago," he said. "I was getting worried."

"I had to make a stop."

Sawyer nodded.

"You going to ask me where?" Robert challenged.

Sawyer cocked his head. "Well, I guess I could. If you'd like me to."

"You don't have to," Robert said.

"Oh, for God's sake, Robert. Talk."

Robert looked over both shoulders. There were other people in the room but nobody was paying them any attention. Tasha was not at her desk.

"I was at the jewelry store."

"You're getting your tongue pierced?" Sawyer asked.

Robert rolled his eyes. "Right. Just as soon as I do yours." He stopped. "I went in thinking I might get a necklace, maybe some matching earrings. Carmen was upset about her car. I thought it might cheer her up."

"Did you find anything?"

Robert tapped his pen on his metal desk. "I got a ring."

"Okay," Sawyer said.

"An engagement ring," Robert clarified. He sat back in his chair and waited for the inquisition to start.

Sawyer didn't say anything, and that made Robert crazy. "Well?" he prompted his friend.

"Congratulations," Sawyer said. "I guess I didn't realize it had gotten to this stage."

"We haven't actually talked about it," Robert admitted.

"What have you talked about?"

"Oh, you know. Favorite ice cream flavors, best movies of the year, spring soaps."

Sawyer raised an eyebrow.

"Never mind. Am I crazy?" Robert asked. "I feel crazy. I feel crazy and light-headed and totally out of control. I swear to God I wasn't planning on buying a diamond ring. It was just a day ago that I was reflecting upon why I'd never get married."

"Marriage is wonderful," Sawyer said.

Robert shook his head. "You've met my mother."

"Yeah, and I like her. Here's a news flash, Robert. You're not your mother."

Robert cupped his chin in his hand. "I know that. But I've spent my whole life determined not to follow in her footsteps. And then suddenly I was inside that jewelry store and it was as if the diamond rings were calling my name. It sounded sort of like, 'Hey, dumb-ass.'"

"You answer to that?"

Robert frowned at him. "Not usually. You know, I was this close to beating the hell out of Frank Sage this morning. Just because I thought he might have painted a white stripe on Carmen's car."

"So that's why you bought a ring?"

Robert shook his head. "I bought a ring because she was sad the other day and I don't want her to ever be sad again. I don't want her to be cold or hungry or to ever worry about money. I want to wrap her in cotton and keep her safe from idiots like Sage. I want…I want to come home to her at night and talk about our days. I want to hold hands at the movies and eat off each other's ice cream spoons." Robert stopped. "I'm losing my mind, aren't I?"

Sawyer smiled. "I knew something was different last night. Tara was doing everything but stand on her head to get your attention and you just looked uncomfortable. I've never seen that before. Not interested, certainly. But never uncomfortable. I thought to myself, where is the cool, calm and collected Robert Hanson who can manage a string of women?"

Robert rolled his eyes. "He got caught in his own fishing line and he's choking."

This time Sawyer laughed. "If it makes you feel any better, you'll be over this in forty or fifty years," he said. "Don't be too hard on yourself. Happens to the best of us."

"I love her," Robert said. "But here's the thing. I don't know how to be a husband and I sure as hell don't know how to be a father. My mother had a parade of men, but none of them were very good at either job. I don't have any role models other than you. And unfortunately, the techniques you're using on Catherine probably aren't the same ones that will be effective with a surly fifteen-year-old boy."

"You're worrying about nothing. You know everything you need to know."

"I hope you're right," Robert said, shaking his head.

"When are you going to pop the question?"

"I have no idea."

"Good plan."

CARMEN STOOD IN Liz's doorway and buttoned her coat. "Have a good night," she said to her friend. "Are you getting out of here soon?"

"Yes. I just called Catherine's sitter and told her I'd be there in about fifteen minutes. What about you?"

"My late appointment canceled so I'm almost done. Just need to stop by Montgomery High School. There's a counselor there who wants to talk with me. She's got a potential referral. I told her I'd stop by on my way home from work."

"You should try to get home before it gets too late. I'm a little freaked out about your car getting vandalized. I know you told me that you don't think Frank Sage had anything to do with it, but the timing is sort of suspect, isn't it?"

Carmen tied her scarf around her neck. "That's certainly the path that Robert seems intent upon following."

Liz smiled. "Yes, Robert. What started with a little pizza at my house seems to be flourishing into something more. You know every time you say his name, your cheeks get pink and there's this look in your eyes that I've never seen before."

Carmen unwound the scarf that she'd just tied. Just thinking about Robert made her warm. "I don't know what's going on," she said honestly. "I am so out of my league here."

"No, you're not," Liz said, waving her hand. "Just let it go where it's going to go. Relax."

"He kissed me," Carmen said.

"I figured as much," Liz said, her tone guarded.

Carmen knew Liz would never ask for details. She was way too classy for that. But then why did she have an adolescent need to give her some?

"It wasn't like a *hey, good friend, nice to see you again* kiss. It was…something. My neighbor saw us in the hallway and I'm not sure I'm going to be able to look her in the eye again."

"Mrs. Curtiss?"

"Yes. I forgot that you'd met her."

"You probably made her day. She's cool now so she was probably really cool when she was your age."

"Yeah, well, I've never been cool. I'm a twenty-nine-year-old woman with the dating skills of a fourteen-year-old."

Liz got up from her desk and walked over to Carmen. She hugged her. "I am so happy for you," she said. "Robert is a great guy. A wonderful friend. What could be better than two of my best friends getting together?"

Carmen shook her head. "There's no hooking up going on here," she said, deliberately using the term that their clients used.

"Well, maybe there should be," Liz said. "Multiple, explosive hookups."

"You're no help," Carmen said, shaking her head in mock disgust. "I have to go. I'll see you tomorrow."

Carmen walked out of OCM and across the street to the parking lot where staff parked. While it wasn't yet dark, the streetlights were on, making the white stripe against the dark paint stand out. The backseat window was covered with duct tape. All in all, it looked pretty bad.

She'd tried to convince Robert that it was random. And she hadn't been blowing smoke. It had to be. Because the idea that somebody disliked her so much that they felt the need to publicly proclaim it was too distasteful.

She'd call tomorrow and see if she could get her car in to get the paint job repaired and the window fixed. It would mean relying on public transportation for a few days, but anything was better than driving this. It looked like an injured skunk on wheels.

Carmen unlocked her door and slid into the cold vehicle. She started the car and shivered while the heater struggled to warm the space. After a couple minutes, she put the car in Drive and pulled out of the lot.

Montgomery School was ten minutes away and then her apartment another ten. She was grateful that no fresh snow had fallen during the day. For once, the streets were pretty good and the traffic not too heavy.

She accelerated toward the green light at the bottom of the hill, only to tap her brakes when it turned yellow.

The pedal went to the floor.

Her brakes were gone. And her car was picking up speed. The light turned red.

She saw the large delivery truck coming from the left, barreling toward the intersection, and knew there was no way they weren't going to collide.

ROBERT WAS PORING through the reports on all the evidence that had been gathered at the scenes where the dead kids had been found, looking for some connection, when his cell phone rang. "Hanson," he answered.

"This is Officer Smith. We met yesterday."

At Carmen's. Good. Maybe they had found some shred of evidence. "What can I help you with?" Robert asked.

"Well, nothing, I guess. I just had some information that I thought you might be interested in."

"Okay."

"The car that was vandalized, well, it was just in an accident. When the responding officer entered the license plate, my name came up. He gave me a call."

Robert shoved back his chair and grabbed his coat. "Where?"

"Corner of Pecan Street and Webster Avenue. Pretty big mess," he added.

"Fatalities?" Robert forced himself to ask.

"No, but the female driver was transported to Mercy Memorial."

Chapter Thirteen

When Robert got to the emergency room, nobody would tell him anything. He pulled his badge and demanded information.

"I'll get a charge nurse," the woman at the desk told him. "I'm not authorized to provide any information."

"Just tell me that she's alive," he said, leaning over the counter.

Either he scared her or she felt sorry for him because she entered a few clicks on her computer. "Alive and stable upon arrival. That's all I can tell you."

It was enough. Carmen was alive. Stable didn't mean that there weren't injuries, even serious ones. But stable was better than all kinds of other potential descriptors that were making his knees weak.

What the hell had happened? He pulled out his cell phone and in minutes had the responding officer on the phone. "This is Detective Hanson. I'm looking for information on the accident that you just processed at the corner of Pecan Street and Webster Avenue. What happened?"

"Female driver, C. Jimenez, driving a dark 2010 Honda blew through the intersection. Back end was clipped by a delivery truck that managed to swerve, or the damage and the injuries would have been significantly worse."

"How badly was she hurt?"

"I don't know. Paramedics were worried about internal injuries. She was conscious, though. Told me that her brakes failed. The lack of skid marks at the scene supports that."

Failed brakes. It happened. But rarely.

Had someone tampered with her car? Deliberately put her at risk? "Where's the vehicle now?"

"It wasn't drivable. We arranged to have it towed to our impound lot so that one of our guys could take a look at it."

"Push it up on the list," Robert instructed. Screw it. Let his boss scream and yell about the importance of not appearing too personally interested in a case.

He wanted blood.

"Will do. Seems like a nice woman, Detective. Kept apologizing for the accident, for causing so many people to have to come out into the cold. Wouldn't get in the ambulance until she'd talked to the driver of the truck, just to make sure he was okay."

Carmen Jimenez was as nice as they came. And she could have easily have been killed today. "Call me the minute you have results."

Robert disconnected and punched Sawyer's number.

"What's up?" Sawyer answered.

"Carmen was in an accident this afternoon. Her brakes failed. She's at Mercy Memorial hospital. Stable condition. I haven't seen her yet."

"Damn," Sawyer hissed.

Robert understood. He knew that Sawyer thought the world of Carmen and that he'd be worried about how Liz would take the news. He also knew that Sawyer wouldn't like the proximity of the danger. If someone was threatening Carmen, then Liz could potentially get caught in the cross fire.

He put his hand into his pocket and ran his fingers across the flat sterling-silver case that held the diamond ring. "I need your help," Robert said.

"Anything."

"Do you know where Carmen parks her car?"

"Yeah. There's a small lot just east of OCM. That's where they all park."

"Okay. Get out there. See if there's anything to suggest that somebody tampered with her car."

"Done."

"I need you to do something else, too. Go find Frank Sage. If he can't account for every minute of his time, arrest him." Yeah, he didn't even know for sure if Carmen's brakes had been tampered with, but he didn't care. He wasn't going to give Sage time to think of an alibi.

"Anything else?"

"Yeah. Tell Liz that I'll call her with an update on Carmen's condition just as soon as I know something." Robert disconnected.

Robert thought about what he should do next. Should he find Raoul? School was out but the kid was probably at band practice. Robert decided to wait. He'd spent the day being pretty irritated with the kid, but there was no doubt that Raoul thought the world of his sister. There was no need to worry him needlessly.

Oh, God, he hoped it would be needless worry. Hoped that somebody would walk out of those doors right now and tell him that everything was *fine.* Just fine.

He went up to the desk again. "I'm still waiting for information on Carmen Jimenez."

The clerk shook her head. "Hang on," she said. She pushed her chair back and walked away. She was back in about two minutes with another woman, ten years older, in blue scrubs with a white lab coat.

"I'm Chelsea Andrews," the woman said. "I'm in charge today. I understand that you're interested in an update on Carmen Jimenez. Is she under arrest, Detective?"

Police business generally took precedence over personal business. "Miss Jimenez is a material witness to a very important ongoing investigation," he said. "I need to talk to her. Now."

"Come with me," she said. "But for what it's worth, the woman has had a hell of a day. I would think the cops would cut her a little slack."

She led him past six closed doors. At the seventh, she stopped and knocked briefly before opening the door.

The exam room was small, with a bed taking up most of the space. Carmen was in a faded blue-and-white gown, in a bed, propped up by two or three pillows.

She had airbag burns across the bridge of her nose and her cheeks. Under her eyes, the skin was red and bruised and he suspected she might have a black eye in a day or two.

She'd still be beautiful. "Hi," he said.

She smiled at him. "I'm not even going to ask how you knew I was here."

He shrugged. "How are you?"

"I'm okay. Lucky," she said, looking at the charge nurse who continued to stand in the doorway. "That's what everybody is telling me."

He reached for her hand. Her skin was warm and he felt himself relax for the first time since he'd received the awful phone call. "Do you have to stay here?" he asked.

"At least until they read the results of the abdominal CT scan. Then I'm hoping to go home."

Robert looked over his shoulder. The charge nurse was frowning at him. "Material witness?" she said, letting her gaze rest on their linked hands.

Robert shrugged and the woman shook her head, turned and left. She closed the door behind her.

Robert leaned over the bed and kissed Carmen. Gently. Sweetly. "I'm so sorry that you're hurt."

"I'm going to be okay," she said, her voice a mere whisper. "It was so scary," she added.

"What happened?"

"I don't know. I mean, I know that I was driving and I saw the light turn yellow. I pushed on the brake and the pedal went to the floor. I knew something was terribly wrong but by then, I was so close to the intersection. There are businesses on both sides. I didn't see anywhere to go." She swallowed hard.

"Then I saw the truck and I really, really thought I was going to die. I pulled my emergency brake and my car went sideways. Then the truck hit me, my air bag went off, and I think I might have blacked out for a minute because the next thing I knew, there was somebody at my door, telling me to just sit tight, that help was coming. I kept asking if anyone else had been hurt and nobody would tell me anything."

"Everybody else is okay," he said. "Don't worry

about that." He hated seeing the look of despair in her pretty brown eyes.

She shook her head. "I just feel horrible. I always maintain my car. I had no idea my brakes were bad. That poor man driving the truck. I finally got to talk to him and he said he was fine but it could have been so much worse and it would have been all my fault."

"Where was your car today?"

"Where it is every day. We park next to the dry cleaner's."

"Any cameras in the lot?"

"I have no idea. There could be, I suppose, but it's a really small lot. Probably only space for six or eight cars." She pushed herself up in the bed. She winced, and he absolutely hated that she was in pain.

"Should I get a nurse?" he asked.

She shook her head. "I'm just a little sore," she said. "I think I got tossed around a little when my car was spinning. Why the questions about where I park?"

He hated that they had to have this conversation, but she needed to understand that the situation had changed today. Until he knew otherwise, he was going to assume that somebody had deliberately tried to harm Carmen. That meant that she needed to be on high alert, cautious of everything and everybody. "Brakes can fail on a car, Carmen. They can. But when brakes go bad, it's usually more of a gradual loss, they get sort of spongy. What you're describing, where there is a total loss of responsiveness, makes me think that there's something else going on here."

"You think somebody messed with my brakes?" She spoke so fast that her words were almost clipped.

"I don't know," he said honestly. "But we will know. Your car got towed to one of our impound lots. I've already talked to somebody about getting it looked at, to figure out what happened."

"This is crazy," she said.

He couldn't argue that. "Sawyer is going to go talk to Frank Sage."

"But—"

He shook his head, stopping her. "And if we find out that someone messed with your car and he can't account for every damn minute of his day, we're going to arrest him."

She didn't try to protest again. He figured that was as good an indication as anything that the past hour had taken a toll on her.

"Why don't you just rest for a few minutes?" he suggested.

She nodded and closed her eyes. He sat by her bed, continuing to gently hold her hand. After a few minutes, her eyes opened again. "Why didn't you go see Frank Sage?" she asked.

He considered what he should tell her and decided to go with the truth. "Because I need to be here. Close enough to touch you, to feel your warm skin, to see the pulse in your neck beat, to hear your breath, to know that you're really okay."

Her eyes widened. He'd surprised her.

He wanted to say more, to explain that he realized it had been just a few days that they'd been spending time together, but that he knew that *this* was something different. Something that he'd never had or felt before.

He wanted to pull the ring out of his pocket, get down on one knee and beg her to marry him.

But he didn't want to have that conversation with her lying in a hospital bed, in a room that anybody could walk into at any minute.

Fortunately, she didn't press. She simply closed her eyes and within a few minutes, her breathing was such that he was pretty sure she'd drifted off to sleep.

He continued to hold her hand, tracing the shape of the delicate bones with the pad of this thumb. It was forty-five minutes before the door opened again. It was the charge nurse. She ignored Robert and gently roused Carmen.

"Ms. Jimenez," she said. "The results of your CT came back normal. No internal injuries."

Carmen smiled, and Robert felt the relief flood his body. She was okay.

"Your ribs are probably going to be sore for a few days so I'd suggest you take it easy. Take some ibuprofen. It's best to try to stay ahead of the pain."

"I can go home?" Carmen asked.

"I'll go get your discharge paperwork ready," the nurse said.

"Thank you," Carmen said. "Everyone here has just been wonderful."

"You're welcome," the nurse said. "I'll be back within fifteen minutes." She left the room.

Carmen smiled at Robert. "Good news," she said.

"Great news," he corrected.

"Yeah." With her free hand, she plucked at the thin sheet that covered her legs. "Time marches on," she said.

"I suppose it does," he said, not sure where she was going.

"Where do you live?" she asked.

He hadn't seen that one coming. "I've got an apartment in one of the high-rises on Lake Shore Drive."

She smiled, a little half smile. "Does it face the lake?"

"It does. On a clear day, I can see fifteen miles out onto Lake Michigan."

"I'll bet that's pretty. Even when it's all iced up, I'll bet it's nice. You know, I used to ice-skate when I was younger."

He got nervous. The CT of the abdomen may have been fine, but maybe they'd missed something. She thought that she'd blacked out for a minute. Was it possible that she'd hit her head? He leaned close and looked at her eyes. Both pupils were the same size.

"I used to do a lot of things. And then I stopped. I got cautious. Told myself that Raoul had lost so much already, that he shouldn't have to lose anything else."

"Honey, I'm not sure—"

"But I think I was just kidding myself. You ever do that, Robert? Kid yourself?"

He was still holding her hand and as unobtrusively as possible, he shifted his hold, then rested his thumb on the inside of her wrist, testing for her pulse. He counted and watched the second hand on the clock for fifteen seconds and multiplied by four. Seventy-two and steady. Skin was warm but not hot. Still, he was just about to call for the nurse to come back. "I'm not sure I'm following you."

"I'd like to see it."

"What?"

"Your apartment."

"Okay," he assured her. "We can make that happen sometime."

"Tonight. Now."

He let go of her hand. "I'm not sure I understand."

She smiled at him. "I'd like to get dressed, get

out of here, go to your apartment and finish what we started in the hallway yesterday morning."

He gripped the bed rail. Her pulse was fine, but his was bucking and heaving. "You've just been in a car accident," he said. "You need to go home and rest. Have some chicken noodle soup. Take a warm bath."

She shook her head.

"What about Raoul?" he asked. Lord, he wanted what she was offering with a vengeance, but the last thing he wanted to face was morning-after regrets.

"He knows nothing about this. He was already expecting me to be home late tonight because I thought I had late clients. I called him a little while ago and told him that I'd be a little later than I expected. He's home, safe, and expects to see me around ten. I'm not planning on spending the night with you, Robert. I thought a couple hours might do it."

He was wound so tight that a couple minutes might take care of it.

"You've thought of just about everything, haven't you?" His voice cracked at the end.

For the first time since he'd seen her lying in the hospital bed, her smile reached her eyes. "You've heard the extent of my ideas. From here on out, we'll have to wing it."

He'd been told he could wing it with the best of

them but it had never mattered more. "You're sure? What about your ribs?"

"Maybe we'll need to be inventive?"

He turned and strode to the door.

"Where are you going?" she asked.

"I'm getting that nurse and we're getting the hell out of here."

Once he was safely in the hallway, he took a minute to compose himself. Then he called Sawyer.

"How's Carmen?" his friend asked.

"She's going to be okay," Robert said.

There was a pause on the other end. "How are you doing?"

He forced himself to chuckle. "I'm okay. You know, if not for the circumstances, I bet you'd be laughing your ass off. Robert Hanson has himself plumb undone over a woman or some other equally nutty Southern saying."

"Plumb undone," Sawyer repeated. "Naw. Smitten. More excited than a hen in a frying pan. Now, that's Southern."

"I'm a little freaked out."

"Of course you are. You're going to be even more freaked out when I tell you that there was a puddle of brake fluid found in the parking lot."

Robert gripped his cell phone. "Sage?"

"I don't think so, buddy. I found him at home, sitting in his easy chair, drinking a beer. I got in his face pretty good until he produced a receipt from his doctor's office. Guess he had to stop in and have some blood work done after work. I was able to verify the time he left his work and when he arrived and left his doctor's office. He wouldn't have had time to disable Carmen's car. I think it was someone else."

"Maybe he paid someone else to do it?" Robert said, unable to forget the animosity he'd seen in Sage's eyes.

"Maybe. But then he's a pretty good actor. I got the feeling he didn't have a clue why I was so interested in his day. I really think it might have been someone else."

That meant that someone else had deliberately tried to hurt Carmen. Why? Who?

He was going to have to tell her. He would.

After.

Chapter Fourteen

It was forty long minutes before an aide came with a wheelchair to escort her out of the emergency room. When they got to the door, Carmen stood up and felt wonderful. She was taking charge of her life.

"How long will it take to get there?" she asked, once she'd gotten settled in his car.

"Fifteen minutes," he said. His jaw was tight.

"Traffic seems pretty light," she said.

He nodded.

"Looks like it might snow again. The nurses were talking about a possibility of four inches."

He didn't answer.

"Is everything okay, Robert?"

"Yes," he said without looking at her.

He was definitely acting odd. "Are you sorry we're doing this?" she asked.

He turned to look at her. "Hell, no."

She smiled. "You seem preoccupied."

"Thoughtful," he said.

Was it possible that she'd put the sexy, confident Robert Hanson off his stride? That was, quite frankly, rather empowering. Exhilarating, really.

But she was going to need a lot more than that to get her through the next couple of hours. "There's something you should probably know," she said.

She didn't hear him sigh, but his chest went up and down in silent anticipation or perhaps, apprehension.

Both might be in order.

"I…uh…haven't had sex for some time."

He nodded and kept his eyes on the road.

"Quite some time, actually," she said.

He turned to look at her. "I don't need details, Carmen."

"Yeah, well, maybe they might be helpful. You see, it's been about thirteen years."

The car jumped forward in a burst of speed. "Sorry," he mumbled.

Sorry I'm a bad driver or sorry I ever agreed to this?

"I guess I just wanted you to know in case…in case I'm not very good at this."

He glanced in his rearview mirror, cut across a lane of traffic and made a sharp left. Then he took a quick right into an underground parking structure. It was dark, and Carmen was grateful for that. Could this get any more embarrassing?

"I'll do my best," she said. She was babbling. Knew it. Couldn't seem to stop. She was so nervous.

"Carmen," he said, his tone kind. "Shut up. Please."

He drove to an empty parking space and pulled in. He shut the car off and opened his door. She sat.

"You can still change your mind," he said, his voice sounding hoarse.

She reached out and opened her door. When he got out, she followed him, staying just a half step behind as he strode into the building. He got into the elevator and punched 34.

He hadn't said another word.

His apartment was at the end of the hallway. He opened the door with a key and motioned her in. The door shut behind him with a final-sounding thud. Across the room, the drapes were open on the big windows and there was a half-moon hanging over the frozen lake. Ice caps sparkled against an expanse of darkness.

She walked across the room and looked down. Lake Shore Drive was lit up and there was still enough evening traffic to make it look interesting.

He walked into the kitchen and flipped on a light above the stove. It was lots of stainless steel and granite counters. There were bar stools with leather seats and lots of art on the walls. There was more leather in the living room and glass tables with nothing on them.

It was beautiful. So different from her apartment with the old furniture, the sagging couch, the sheet music lying everywhere.

What the hell had she been thinking? They couldn't be any more different. He was a handsome, single guy living an upscale kind of life in an upscale kind of place. She was a tired counselor, raising her fifteen-year-old brother and over the years had adopted his attitude that they were cool if they put tomato and bacon on their grilled cheese sandwiches.

"Maybe—"

He put his finger to her lip, silently shushing her. "Would you like something to drink?" he asked. "Some wine, perhaps?"

She shook her head. He wasn't going to get a chance to shush her a third time.

He smiled. "Would you like to see the rest of the apartment?"

This time she nodded.

He motioned for her to precede him down the short hallway. There was a bathroom that looked as if no one had ever used it. The soap was new and the towels were fresh.

Next, there was a room that looked part office, part workout room. There was a treadmill and a rowing machine and some hand weights. There was also a desk and glory be, there were actually a few files on it and a rogue stapler had found its way out of a drawer.

There was only one door left. It was partially closed. He reached over her shoulder to open it. It faced the lake, as the living room had. And here the drapes were also pulled open, letting in moonlight and the reflection of city lights.

It was a large room, yet still the bed took up a great deal of it. It had to be a king, and the padded headboard added to its overall mass. She was pretty sure that if she sat on it, her feet might not touch the ground.

It was a far cry from the little double bed in her twelve-by-twelve bedroom.

The bed was made. It had a thick gray duvet. Several gray and purple pillows were tossed on a big leather chair in the corner of the room. It made her want to smile. He was neat enough to make his bed but he wasn't going to mess with pillows.

They'd probably been a gift from some girlfriend.

And he didn't want to hurt her feelings so he likely tossed them back on the bed every time she visited.

She wasn't going to kid herself that she was the first woman who'd spent a few hours here. She wouldn't even be the last.

But tonight she was the woman who was going to lie on the gray duvet with a man who made her literally crazy with need. That was enough. She was going to celebrate life. Celebrate the ability to touch and feel.

Robert walked across the room to a door in the far corner. He flipped on a light and she could tell that it was another bath. He closed the door most of the way, allowing just a little of the light to come into the room.

"Is this okay?"

She shrugged.

He raised one dark eyebrow but didn't say anything. He took off his coat and gloves and tossed them over the pillows in the chair.

"May I take your coat?" he asked.

She slowly peeled her gloves off and put them in the pockets of her blue cape. Then she took off her scarf, then the cape. She tossed them all to him.

He caught them, walked over to the chair, and more carefully laid them on top of his own outerwear. He walked back to the bed and sat on it. He was facing the window.

She continued to stand near the door.

He patted the bed next to him. "Care to have a seat?"

She walked over to the bed and sat down, making sure there was a good foot between them. She was right. Her feet didn't touch the floor. She clasped her hands together and rested them in her lap.

He didn't say anything for a minute. Finally, he turned to her. "I'm sorry I told you to shut up."

"I was babbling," she said, accepting his apology. She'd wanted to tell herself to shut up.

"You were nervous," he said. He reached out a big hand and covered her clasped hands.

"Am nervous," she clarified.

"I am, too," he said, smiling at her.

She rolled her eyes. "Oh, please. I don't think it's been thirteen years since you had a woman stay over."

With his thumb, he stroked her wrist. "That's true," he said. "And if I tell you that this is different, you're probably not going to believe me." He hesitated. "So I'm not going there. But what I want you to know is that I want you so much that I'm scared to death that I'm going to blow this. That I'm going to move too fast or do something that you don't like and you're going to be sorry that you ever came here."

His voice cracked at the end. That, and the look in his eyes, gave her the courage to reach out, to stroke the side of his face with the palm of her hand. "I want to be here. With you."

"Why?" he asked, staring in her eyes. "You've waited a long time. Why now? Why me?"

Because I think I love you. Maybe ever since you poured the M&M'S in my popcorn and said we had to get married. "I could have died today. I didn't want to die without this."

"I guess I'm glad I could be of assistance," he said, sounding a little irritated.

She let it go. Better he think that he was a convenient hookup. Otherwise, he'd probably be scared enough to take a leap out of the thirty-fourth-floor window.

"Would you kiss me now?" she asked.

He leaned in. His mouth was warm and heavy and she could feel her cold bones start to melt. He pushed his tongue in her mouth and when she sucked on it, he groaned.

And then he wrapped an arm around her shoulders and gently pulled her down onto the pretty gray duvet that covered the big soft bed.

He kissed her for a very long time and she could feel other parts of her body come out of hibernation and begin to beg for attention. Her skin felt warm and extra sensitive. Her breasts, heavy.

She reached up to unbutton his shirt. He stilled her hands. "Not quite yet," he said softly.

He slipped his hand under her shirt and traced her ribs gently with the pad of his thumb. "You're sure you're not too sore?" he asked.

"Sure," she said and settled back into his kisses.

His hand traveled upward and when he encountered only skin, he lifted his head.

She smiled. "My bra is in my purse. I didn't put it back on at the hospital."

She heard a low growl and reveled in the feel of his broad hand holding her breast, caressing it. He gently pinched her nipple and sparks shot through her.

Her body had moved from anticipation to full-blown engagement. She pressed against him. He was hard. Sinfully hard.

Another growl and this time he lightly bit at her bottom lip. "You're not playing fair," he said.

"I've waited a long time," she said.

"And you'll have to wait just a few minutes longer. You're a fine wine, Carmen. Meant to be sipped, savored, enjoyed."

And he did just that. Her shirt came off, then her slacks and panties, and there wasn't a part of her that wasn't kissed, stroked, sucked or loved. When he spread her legs and touched her with his tongue, she responded with an explosive orgasm that left her panting and a little embarrassed that she might have squeezed his poor head with her thighs.

"Did I hurt you?" she asked.

He lifted his head. "You were perfect," he said.

"Even if that's all there is," she said, "it's the best sex I ever had."

"That's not all there is," he said. Then he rolled her underneath him and proceeded to prove his point not once, but twice.

ROBERT FELT THE mattress shift and in one quick movement, Carmen slipped from the bed. He could have stopped her but he knew it was time for her to go home.

Damn. He wanted her to stay. Had loved having her in his bed, in his arms, under his body.

Loved.

He loved Carmen Jimenez. But was she ready to hear that?

He watched her pull on her clothes. She'd turned, giving him her back. He was grateful for the moon. It gave enough light that he could see the delicate ridge of her spine, the sexy muscles in her upper back, her gently rounded shoulders.

Her skin had been so soft, smelled so good.

Now her pants, shirt.

"I'll drive you," he said, throwing off the covers.

"I can catch a cab," she said, pulling on her sweater.

He moved behind her and wrapped his arms around her. Her long hair brushed against his chest. He gathered it up in his fist and pulled it to the side. He kissed the back of her neck. She stilled.

"Don't be ridiculous," he murmured, moving his lips close to her ear. "Thank you," he added. He could feel his body reacting to their closeness, wanting her again.

"You're welcome," she said, amusement in her tone. She moved away. "I really do need to get home."

Resigned, he started pulling on his own clothes. When he got to his pants, the ring in his pocket felt heavy against his thigh.

Should he ask her?

What if she said no? The night had been perfect. One that he would remember forever. Could he take the chance of ruining it?

It wasn't a conversation he wanted to have when she was hurrying to get home. Maybe this weekend. That might be nice. He pulled on his coat and less than five minutes later, they were in his cold car, driving toward her apartment. It had started to snow and the streets were slick. She was quiet and spent the time looking out her window.

Did she regret the past two hours?

That caused a sharp pain to slice across his chest. "What are you thinking?" he asked, even though he wasn't sure he was strong enough to hear the answer.

"I wish I knew more about cars."

Well, that wasn't what he'd expected. "Why?"

"I'm going to need to buy a new one. It would save me some time if I had some idea of what I wanted. Or what I could afford," she added.

"Don't worry about it," he said.

"I've got a little money saved," she said. "I guess I'll just have to wait until I hear from the insurance company."

He could hear the worry in her voice and it made

him so angry. This was a woman who already had her share of worries. She didn't need another one. "Carmen, it doesn't matter what your insurance pays. Whatever extra you need, I'll give it to you."

She didn't say anything for two long blocks. Finally, she turned in her seat. "As payment?" she asked, her tone hard.

He almost wrecked his damn car. "I don't even know how you could suggest that."

"I'm sorry," she said, looking down at her gloved hands. "I don't know where that came from. I guess I'm still not sure why a guy like you would want to be with a woman like me. I'm not your type, Robert."

There was no place to pull over the car but there was no traffic either, so he simply slowed down. Moving at a snail's pace, he drove with one hand and reached for her with his other. He wrapped an arm around her shoulder and pulled her close.

"The past two hours of my life have been the best two hours that I've ever had," he said. "And based on those two hours, I'd say you're exactly my type."

Her face was sort of muffled by his coat but he could feel her nod her head. Five minutes later he pulled up to her apartment.

"I think it might be better if I go in alone," she said. "Less questions from Raoul and all."

"Just tell me that we're okay, Carmen."

She leaned across the car and kissed his cheek. "It's all good, Robert. Thank you so much."

"Okay. Then I have one more thing to tell you. When I talked to Sawyer earlier, he confirmed that there was a puddle of brake fluid in your parking lot. Then, while we were at the apartment, I got a text. Your brake lines were definitely tampered with. Looks like somebody took a hacksaw and cut through both the front and back lines." He stopped, letting her absorb the information.

"So, it was deliberate?" she said, her tone flat. "Someone deliberately tried to harm me, maybe even kill me."

"Looks that way."

She turned to him, her dark eyes big. "Who would do something like that?"

"I don't know. We don't think it was Sage. He's got an alibi." He waited for her to throw out an *I told you so* but she said nothing. "We're going to need a list of all your clients."

"Jamison won't go for that," she said.

"Your boss almost lost OCM last year to a bomber. I think he's developed a healthy respect for working with the law. Besides, he cares about you."

She nodded. "He still won't be happy. I'm not happy. I just can't see it being any of them. I help them. They know it."

"Family members then?"

She shrugged. "Maybe." She looked at her watch. "Speaking of family, I better get inside." She looked up. "What if Raoul had been with me today? What if he'd been injured because someone has a grudge against me? I couldn't bear it, Robert."

He started to pull her close again, but she resisted.

"I have to go," she said. "I need to talk to Raoul. He needs to understand what's going on. We both need to be watching."

"How are you going to get to work in the morning? I could swing by and give you a lift."

She shook her head. "Thank you, but no. A cab will work just fine." She opened her door.

He opened his. When she started to object, he held up a hand. "Give me a break here, Carmen. At least let me walk you to your door."

She smiled. "I'm not used to having someone do things for me."

"Yeah, well, I hope you're the type that adjusts to change quickly."

RAOUL WAS ALREADY in bed when he heard the apartment door open. He glanced at his clock. Carmen had worked really late.

He heard footsteps in the hallway and then a knock on his door. "Hi, sis," he said.

She came in and kissed him on the forehead, like

she used to do when he was a little kid. "How was your day?" she asked.

He didn't think the cop had told her about his visit to the school and the conversation about Speedy's. He knew his sister. She would not have waited until ten o'clock to have a conversation with him. "Pretty good," he said. "Band practice went better," he added, because she was always interested in that.

"Just a few more days until the concert," she said.

"Yeah. Thursday at seven. I have to wear black pants and a white shirt."

"No problem. Hey, do you have a minute?"

He was in bed. "I guess."

"I had some bad luck today," she said. "This morning, when I was leaving for work, I discovered that somebody had vandalized my car. They painted a white strip along the side of it and broke out the backseat window."

Oh, man. It was going to be embarrassing riding around in something like that.

"Can we get it fixed?"

"Of course. But that's not all. This afternoon, when I was driving to an appointment, my brakes went out. I couldn't stop for a red light and another vehicle hit me."

He sat up and jammed pillows behind his back. "Are you okay?"

"I am. Got checked out at the hospital and everything is just fine. But here's the thing, Raoul. The police think that somebody cut my brake lines. Somebody wanted me to get in an accident."

That didn't make any sense. Everybody loved Carmen.

Raoul felt a pain in his stomach. Everybody didn't love him. JJ and Beau hated him. They also knew where he lived and the kind of car his sister drove. Were they crazy enough that they would have spray painted her car and then messed with the brakes?

The pain became sharper when he realized that he'd just recently had a conversation about Carmen with somebody. With Apollo.

If the guy was crazy enough to shoot up a car lot, then he was probably crazy enough to cut some brake lines. It didn't make sense because Apollo had said that he was a friend of Hector's. But maybe he'd been lying. Maybe he'd been nice to Raoul just so that he could get close to Carmen? He seemed to be about Carmen's age. Maybe they'd gone to school together? Maybe she'd turned him down for a date or something and he'd been pissed for a long time and was finally getting his revenge?

Raoul's head was spinning. Maybe his sister had almost died because of him. He wanted to tell her about JJ and Beau and about Apollo but he knew how disappointed she'd be that he hadn't told her the truth before. And when she found out about Speedy's, she would be crazy mad.

"What are you going to do?" he whispered.

"Keep living my life. And that's what you're going to do, too. But we're going to be a little more careful, a little more watchful, until we figure this out. Okay?"

He nodded and reached his arms out to hug her. She looked surprised and he realized that it had been a long time since he'd hugged his sister.

She grabbed him tight and hung on. "It will be okay, Raoul. I promise."

It would. He was going to make sure of that.

Chapter Fifteen

Tuesday

Robert was at his desk by six. He made fresh coffee because the guys who had worked overnight evidently liked drinking mud. He was standing in the break area, waiting for the toaster to pop up his bagel, when Lieutenant Fischer came in. He nodded at Robert.

"You're in early," his boss said.

Robert nodded and reached for the cream cheese packet. "You, too."

"Yeah. My wife said she could take the kids to school this morning."

That reminded Robert of his conversation with Judy Franconi Wright. "Henry Wright was getting recruited by Stalwart Academy. That's what his mom told me when I saw her on Sunday."

His boss cocked his head. "Recruited? That school never recruits. It's a competitive application process with pretty good transparency."

Robert's stomach felt weird and he was pretty sure it wasn't because his bagel was still on the counter. "You're sure?"

The man nodded.

Robert pulled his notebook out of his shirt pocket and started flipping through pages. "Here it is. Stalwart Academy. Said that some representative had been talking to Henry for the last couple of weeks. He was very excited—evidently music was his life. But she didn't know the guy's name. Wanted Henry to get his business card but he never brought it home. She felt bad because she was wondering if the man knew Henry was dead."

He met his boss's eyes. "Maybe this is it. Maybe this is the thread that we've been looking for. I'm going to that school."

"If they give you any trouble, drop my name. In addition to the tuition, I just made a nice donation to their new music room."

Robert was anxious but still he drove carefully. The snow that had started falling last night when he'd been making love to Carmen had continued on through the middle of the night and there had to be at least five fresh inches. Fortunately, it had stopped in time for the plows to clear most of the main roads, although the side streets probably wouldn't all get plowed until much later in the day.

When he got to the school, it was not quite

seven. He pressed the buzzer on the outside door and waited.

"Yes?" It was a woman but she was hard to hear over the static.

He looked up at the camera that was pointed toward him. "Detective Robert Hanson of the Chicago Police. I need to speak with somebody in charge."

He heard a buzz and pulled open the door. There was an arrow on the wall, indicating that the office was to his right. He walked into the small administrative area and could smell flavored coffee. There were two women sitting at desks. One had a phone to her ear, and he heard enough to figure out that she was talking to somebody about a kid being ill and missing school. The other woman smiled at him.

"It's pretty early, Detective," she said.

"I wanted to catch someone before the day started." There was no need to tell this woman that time was running out. Tomorrow was Wednesday. "I need to talk to someone about one of your recruitment representatives."

She cocked her head to the left. "I've only been here a month. I'm filling in for someone who is on maternity leave. But I guess I didn't realize that we had recruitment representatives." She looked at the other woman, but she was still on the phone. "I suppose you could talk to Assistant Principal Bryant. She's the only administrator who has arrived. I'll go get her."

"Perfect," he said. In less than three minutes, the woman was back, this time followed by another woman.

Assistant Principal Bryant was mid-thirties, and had blond hair that fell straight to her shoulders and a knockout figure. She wore a classy white wool suit with boots that came up to her knee.

He was reminded of what Carmen had said. *I'm not your type.* Well, if he had a type, this woman was it.

And he felt nothing when she shook his hand.

"What can I do for you, Detective?" Her tone was friendly.

"I am investigating the murder of Henry Wright. He was the young man who was killed last week."

"Of course," she said. "I read about it in the newspaper."

"I understand that someone from your school had made contact with Henry in the last couple of weeks to discuss his possible attendance here next year."

She tapped her index finger against her bottom lip in thought. Her polished fingernails were nicely shaped. There was no wedding ring. "I suppose it's possible that he knew one of our teachers outside of school and they had some conversation about what it's like to attend Stalwart Academy."

"No," Robert said. "That wasn't the way it was explained to me. Someone from Stalwart Academy had made contact with him specifically to discuss the possibility of a freshman scholarship."

She smiled. "I can guarantee you that didn't happen. Stalwart Academy doesn't have to recruit," she said somewhat smugly. "We have a waiting list of candidates every year. And we certainly don't offer any scholarships."

It was exactly what Lieutenant Fischer had thought. He stood up. "Thank you for your time."

She had a stack of business cards on her desk and she reached for one. She flipped it over and wrote a number on the back. "My pleasure, Detective Hanson. Here's my card and my personal cell phone on the back, in the event that you'd want to follow up. On anything."

The message was clear. She was interested.

He put the card in his pocket. He wasn't.

THE BUS WAS ten minutes late and by the time it dropped him off at his corner, Raoul had to run the last two blocks to make it to band practice on time. He didn't want to be late. With the winter concert only two days away, his teacher was acting crazy about that kind of stuff. He was practically on school grounds when Apollo stepped out of the bushes.

"Hey," Raoul said, stopping fast. For the past twenty-four hours, ever since Robert Hanson had shown up at his school, demanding to know about

Speedy's, he'd been worried sick about what he'd done. Every time he heard a siren in the distance, he'd envisioned that it was the cops coming to get him.

All the trouble had started with this guy. "I'm late," Raoul said.

"No worries," Apollo said. "I remembered that I had one more thing of Hector's that he wanted you to have."

"What?" Raoul asked.

Apollo held up both gloved hands. "Can't say, can't say. But it's a big deal. What time does your band practice start tomorrow?"

"There's no practice tomorrow morning. Our band teacher has a meeting."

Apollo smiled. "Good. Then meet me here this time tomorrow. That will give me plenty of time to show you and you can still get to school on time like a good boy."

Raoul didn't like Apollo's attitude. "Hey, my sister was in a car accident yesterday. You don't happen to know anything about that, do you?"

Apollo frowned at him. "No. Why should I?"

Because you're a creep. "I don't know. I just had to ask."

"Raoul, I only want what Hector wanted for you. Now, meet me tomorrow. You'll be glad you did."

He would meet him but that was the last he was going to have anything to do with him. He might have been Hector's friend at one time but there was something Raoul didn't like about him.

"I'll think about it," he said.

"On Wednesday," Apollo said before he disappeared back into the snow-covered bushes.

CARMEN HAD BEEN at her desk for less than ten minutes when her office phone rang. "Carmen Jimenez," she answered.

"Hey, just checking to make sure you made it to work okay."

Robert. Just thinking about him made her warm. She hadn't showered before bed. Hadn't wanted to wash away his scent. Instead, she'd gone to bed naked, something she never did, especially not on a cold winter night. But she'd lain naked in her double bed and imagined what it would be like if Robert was next to her with his warm skin, his strong muscles, his talented fingers and mouth.

It was almost embarrassing and certainly not something she intended to share with Robert. "Yes, got here just a little while ago. I asked Raoul to text me when he got to school and he's also safe and sound."

"Good." He paused. "Can I see you tonight?"

"I don't want to leave Raoul home alone," she said.

"Of course. I could stop by. It would probably be late anyway. He goes to sleep at some point, right?"

Was she ready to have a man in the apartment? Raoul was a heavy sleeper, but what if he somehow overheard them? What if he knocked on the door?

She needed to talk to him first. Maybe she could do that at dinner?

"I'm not sure, Robert. I want to. But I have to handle this carefully."

"I know. I can respect that. But there's something that I want to ask you."

"About?"

"Let's just wait until tonight."

He clearly didn't want to talk about it now. "I'll call you later and let you know if it's okay to come over," she said.

WHEN ROBERT GOT back to the station, he made fast tracks to where Blaze, Wasimole and Sawyer were having a heated discussion. He could see the frustration on their faces.

"I think I've got something," he said.

All three of them looked up. Blaze and Wasimole looked exhausted; Sawyer looked interested.

He filled them in on his conversation with Judy Franconi Wright and his more recent conversation with Assistant Principal Bryant. When he finished, he rubbed his cold hands together. "Somebody made contact with Henry Wright just weeks before he died. Somebody that we know now wasn't legit. We need to go back to the families of the other three victims and see if we can find a similar thread."

Wasimole and Blaze nodded. "We can take Johnnie Whitmore and Ben Johanson, victims one and two."

"Okay. We'll take Gabe Monroe. I never did get to talk to his parents, just the grandmother. Hopefully they will be back from vacation."

Blaze was walking away when she turned. "Let's try to circle back together early afternoon." She didn't need to say anything else. Time was getting the best of them. Wednesday was now less than eighteen hours away.

"Okay," Robert said.

On the way out of the building, Sawyer eyed him. "Anything you want to tell me?" he said.

"No," Robert answered.

Sawyer rolled his eyes. "I'm not looking for details, idiot. I know you planned on taking Carmen home from the hospital. How is she?"

Fabulous. Sexy as hell. Inexperienced in a wonderful way. "She said her ribs are a little sore but she got lucky. Real lucky."

"Lieutenant Fischer assigned it to Vance. He's a good cop. He'll figure it out if there's anything there."

"I know. I sent him a text last night asking who he was going to assign it to. Vance is a good choice. I'd have been a better one."

"You'd have been the worse one. Plenty of motivation but not a lot of credibility when it came time for a trial. *Yes, Judge, I am sleeping with the victim.* That never goes over well."

Sawyer was right. It still didn't make him happy.

"So, did you ask her?" Sawyer asked.

"No. Yesterday was absolutely crazy. Maybe tonight. I told her I wanted to talk to her about something."

"You'll know when it's the right time. Come on, let's go talk to Maury and Carol Monroe."

WHEN THEY GOT to the Monroe home, there was no grandmother this time. Maury answered the door. He was wearing dress slacks and a nice shirt, and he had a cell phone in his hand.

"Detectives Montgomery and Hanson," Robert said as they flashed identification. "I stopped by last week and spoke with your mother. She said you were out of town. I know we didn't have an appointment but we were hoping we could spend a little time with you and your wife today."

"My wife isn't here. She ran to the grocery store," he said.

"Do you have a few minutes?" Robert asked.

"Sure. We just got home a little while ago." He led them into the living room. There was a young woman on the couch holding the ugly dog. Robert guessed her age at about sixteen.

"This is my daughter, Trina," Maury said.

He and Sawyer took chairs. Maury sat on the couch next to his daughter.

Robert remembered that the grandmother had indicated that the sister was having a hard time. "Maybe your daughter would want to do something else for a little while," he suggested.

Maury looked at his daughter, and she shook her head violently. He patted her leg. "She stays. She feels that she's been left out of discussions about her brother and that makes her angry."

Information was a funny thing. Everybody wanted it until they heard something they wished they hadn't. But it wasn't his decision.

"We are wondering if during the weeks prior to his death, if Gabe had mentioned meeting anyone new? Maybe someone from a school or something like that?"

Maury shook his head. "He talked about kids sometimes that I didn't know, but I don't think anybody was really new. Just his classmates. I think you guys already looked at his computer and his Facebook page."

Blaze and Wasimole had secured that immediately after the killing. There was nothing on there that made them believe that he had met up with someone. "Where did Gabe hang out after school?" Sawyer asked.

"He usually came home, watched some television, played video games." Maury looked at his daughter. "Right?"

She nodded. "Sometimes he came to band practice with me. Mr. Reynolds didn't care if he watched."

Robert looked up from his notepad. "You play the drums, right?"

"Yeah. Gabe used to screw around with them all the time," she said. "It used to make me so mad."

And now, Robert could tell, she felt bad about that.

"Have you ever heard of the Gottart Studio?"

She shook her head. "I'm not sure. When I was at band camp last year, a couple other kids were talking about taking lessons somewhere. That might have been the place."

"Band camp?" Robert asked. "What's that?"

"It's the citywide camp at Grant Park. It's huge. Gabe went with me a couple days. He hung out in the park while I was practicing. I remember I came back from lunch one day and I caught him sitting behind my drums pretending that they were his. I told him to get lost." Her eyes filled with tears. "I told him that a lot."

Maury patted his daughter's leg again.

Robert pulled out his cell phone and sent a quick text to Blaze. *See if either of the victims attended the citywide band camp at Grant Park last summer.*

"Do you recall anything unusual happening at band camp?" Robert asked, hating that he had to push the girl. "Did Gabe get to know any of the other attendees when he was hanging around?"

"I don't know," she said. "It's just a bunch of kids and you get paired up with people that you don't even know. The teachers are usually okay. Most of them are music teachers from either middle school or high school. There was one guy that was sort of a dork and he may have talked to Gabe. I wasn't paying attention."

"That's fine," Robert assured her. "You've been extraordinarily helpful. Really."

They left the Monroes and immediately headed toward Henry Wright's house. They knocked and when Judy answered, Robert was relieved to see a cup of coffee in her hand. He introduced Sawyer, and they sat.

"We'll only take a minute of your time. I know you told me that your son played the cornet. Do you recall if he attended band camp last summer at Grant Park? The citywide camp?"

She nodded. "Of course. That was his third year. I told you. He was very talented."

"Of course. Did he ever talk about anybody that he met at camp?"

She shook her head. "Not that I recall. I used to pick him up and there were kids everywhere."

WITHIN THE HOUR, Blaze had confirmed that both Johnnie Whitmore and Ben Johanson had attended the citywide band camp. The air in the station fairly hummed with energy. It was the first solid link among all four victims.

They'd discovered that while it was generally referred to as a citywide band camp, it was really hosted by a corporation out of Dallas, Texas, that put on similar events across the country. Schools helped distribute the information to students, payment was made directly to the company, and it subsequently secured space and staff to run the program. The company employed very few staff members on a full-time basis. Most were simply contracted locally for the three weeks that the camp lasted. It was good extra money for teachers who didn't work in the summers.

When they'd spoken to the senior administrator whose office was in Dallas, he'd assured them they would drop everything to prepare a list of attendees, teachers and all other staff.

"Come on, come on." Robert drummed his fingers on the desk and waited for Blaze to tell them that the list had come in her email.

It was two o'clock before they had anything of substance. The first list had over four hundred kids' names. The second list had the names of sixteen teachers. The detectives set aside the first list. The person who had contacted Henry Wright had posed as a representative of Stalwart Academy. He had to have appeared to be an adult or it wouldn't have been believable. There were ten men and six women on the list.

They didn't worry about the women.

These crimes had been brutal and would have required some strength to move the bodies. There were women who had that kind of strength but when time was short, you played the odds. Plus Judy Franconi Wright had said that her son referred to the recruitment representative as *he*.

"You and Sawyer take these five," Blaze said, handing Robert a list. "Wasimole and I'll take the rest."

The list had included the home address. They probably had that for tax forms. That was helpful. However, it did not have the school where the teacher worked.

Robert drove to the first address, that of a Mr. Burt Willow, while Sawyer worked the phone, trying to get all the information he could about the people on the list.

Everyone was working as fast as they could. Robert only hoped it would be fast enough.

Chapter Sixteen

"Hey look, it's Limpy."

Raoul didn't turn around. Damn. All he wanted was to get to band practice. One more hallway and he'd have been safe.

He was sick of these jerks. And he wasn't taking it anymore. Plus, he wanted some answers about Carmen's car.

He veered to his left, pushed hard on the crash bar of the exterior door, and was outside. He didn't stop to put his coat on. Instead, he carried it, stuffed under his arm. He had his backpack slung over that same shoulder and he carried his trombone case in his other hand.

The sidewalks were empty. He started walking faster. Footsteps, harsh against the concrete sidewalk, chased him. He smiled. These guys were in for the surprise of their lives.

He turned, holding his trombone in front of him.

"We been looking for you," JJ said.

"You're not avoiding us, are you?" Beau asked.

Raoul shook his head.

"How's your trumpet?"

"It's a trombone," Raoul said. "There's a difference. But you guys are probably too stupid to know that."

"Trombone. Ooh, la la." JJ pushed him on the shoulder and he fell back a couple steps.

"Stop it," he said.

JJ pushed again. And again. And Raoul let himself get propelled into the long alley that separated the block.

Beau pointed to a Dumpster about twenty feet away. "Last time he crawled down the hall like a dog. And don't dogs get their dinner out of the Dumpster?" He grabbed Raoul's right arm.

Raoul let his coat fall to the ground but he kept his backpack on his shoulder.

JJ opened the lid and pulled out three white garbage sacks. He ripped open the top of all three, dumping the contents on the ground.

Raoul thought he might get sick just from smelling it. Dirty diapers and food and wet newspapers. All kinds of other stuff he couldn't even identify.

Beau put both hands on Raoul's shoulders and pushed him down to his knees. "Get down, dog. Eat your dinner." Again he shoved Raoul, causing him to lose his balance. His shoulder hit the ground. Icy gravel surrounded the garbage container and it hurt.

The boys laughed, pushing each other around. "You know what my dog does?" said JJ. "He likes to roll around. Start rolling, doggy." He kicked Raoul in the stomach so hard it took Raoul's breath away.

Another kick. "Roll."

Raoul rolled in the garbage. He rolled back. Over and over again. Until the boys tired of the game.

Beau grabbed the back of his collar and lifted him up. "Don't make us come looking for you," he said. "Now give us your money."

"It's in my backpack," Raoul said.

"Then get it out. We don't have all day."

Raoul unzipped his backpack and pulled out the ten-dollar bill that Carmen had given to him that morning. "Here," he said.

"That's better," JJ said. He put the money in his pocket and started to walk away. Beau fell into step next to him.

Raoul reached into his backpack again and pulled out his gun. He stood up. The boys paid no attention to him. After all, he was just a little kid.

He held his arms out, both hands around the gun, just as Apollo had taught him. "Hey," he yelled.

Both boys turned, laughing. They stopped when they saw the gun.

"It's never going to stop, is it?" Raoul said, walking toward them. Wet newspaper clung to his pants. His arms, cut by the sharp rocks, bled. He didn't care.

"Come on, man. We were just having some fun. Put your gun away," JJ said, edging back a step.

"You're both just stupid jerks," Raoul yelled, waving his gun from one to the other.

They didn't move.

Raoul took another step toward them. His arms started to shake. They had to pay. The sons of bitches had to pay.

BURT WILLOW LOOKED about seventy. His apartment was at the end of a long, narrow hallway. He answered the door with the newspaper in his hand. He was probably five-two and a hundred and twenty pounds.

"May I help you?"

"Detectives Hanson and Montgomery," Robert said. They showed him their badges. "We understand that you were an instructor at the citywide band camp last year."

He smiled and his teeth were in better shape than the rest of his body. "For the past eight years. Ever since my wife died. Love those kids."

Sawyer and Robert made eye contact. Willow wasn't physically strong enough to be their guy. But maybe he could help.

"We're trying to identify a couple people who were there," Sawyer said.

The man shook his head. "There are hundreds of kids. It would be hard to remember a couple."

"We're more interested in the staff," Sawyer clarified. "Did you know the other instructors?"

The man nodded. "Most of us had been teaching at the camp for years. Of course, every year there were a couple new folks. Most were real nice."

"Most?" Robert asked.

The man appeared uncomfortable. "Well, I don't like to talk bad about people. Never know when the good maker is going to call me up and I don't want my last deed to be something like that."

"Mr. Willow, this is important," Robert said. He nodded toward the newspaper that the man had folded under this arm. "Have you been following the story of the suspected serial killer?"

He nodded. "Of course. Terrible thing."

"We have reason to believe that all four of the victims were at last year's citywide band camp. Three played instruments and one was there visiting his sister who played."

He didn't respond, but Robert could tell that the news startled him. Robert didn't waste time. He reached into his shirt pocket and pulled out the list of instructor names. "Can you take a look at this list and identify the individuals who were new?"

Mr. Willow studied it. He pointed to a name. "This guy."

Barry Taylor. Excellent. Robert rubbed his hands together. "Anybody else?"

Mr. Willow ran a long finger down the list, then he did it a second time. It took everything Robert had not to grab the list and run out the door.

Time wasn't their friend.

It was already almost four.

"I think this was the other new guy."

Douglass Sparrow.

"You'd have thought the two of them might forge a friendship but they were both loners. Just odd ducks."

They were almost back to their car when Robert's cell phone rang. He saw the number and his heart did some kind of funny spin in his chest.

"Hi, Carmen," he said.

"Are you busy?" she asked.

He could hear the tension in her voice. "What's wrong?" he asked.

"I just got a call from Raoul's school. He's not at band practice. Their winter concert is Thursday night and if a kid misses this week, they don't get to play in the concert. He's first chair and the band director really wants him at the concert. I think that's why he made the extra effort to call my cell phone."

"And you know that he went to school today?"

"We left at the same time. And remember, he sent me a text telling me he'd arrived."

"Okay. Are you still at work?"

"No. I was in a cab on my way back to the office when the call came in. I tried a couple times to reach Raoul on his cell phone. When that didn't work, I couldn't go back to the office. Plus, I was less than ten minutes from my house. I was so sure that he'd be here."

"Were there any signs that he'd returned to the apartment at some point during the day?"

"No."

"Kids skip school stuff all the time," Robert said. "It's probably not a big deal."

There was a pause on the other line.

"Carmen?" he prompted.

"I searched his room. I found a box of bullets in his bottom drawer."

Speedy's Used Cars. He was surer than ever that the kid had been lying. What the hell else had he been lying about? "He has a gun?"

"Not that I know about," she said, her voice cracking. "It's not in his room. It's not in this apartment. I've looked everywhere."

He could tell she was close to tears. "Okay, honey. Don't worry. I'll go find him," Robert said.

"Just bring him home safe, Robert. That's all I ask."

Robert hung up, hoping like hell he wouldn't have to disappoint her.

"What's up?" Sawyer asked.

Robert explained the situation.

"Go," said Sawyer. "I've got this. You should probably start looking near his school. On the way there, you can drop me off and I'll grab my own car. I'll go check out Barry Taylor. We'll reconnect once you've found Raoul."

"I'm going to find him, right?" Robert asked. He could show his friend the fear that he'd had to hide from Carmen.

"You will. You're the best damn cop I know, Robert. If you can't find him, nobody can."

AFTER ROBERT DROPPED off Sawyer, he sped toward Mahoney High. School had been out for about twenty minutes. If Raoul had decided to duck out of band practice, then he could be several blocks away. Of course, if he'd gotten on a bus, then all bets were off. He could be anywhere.

Robert debated whether he should broadcast Raoul's description. Certainly more eyes looking for the kid was better, but the whole thing about Speedy's Used Cars stopped him from doing that. He didn't want any of his fellow cops looking too closely at Raoul right now.

He drove up and down the streets that would have been the logical ones for Raoul to have taken if he'd decided to walk home, all too aware that there was less than an hour of good daylight left.

Once it got darker, it would be so much harder to find him.

Damn kid.

It was another ten minutes before he heard something come across the car radio that sparked his interest. He turned up the volume. Report of kids fighting in an alley. Between Parker Street and Venture Avenue.

Less than two blocks away.

Robert flipped on his lights but no siren.

When he got to the entrance of the alley, his heart almost stopped.

Raoul was standing in the middle of the icy alley and he had a gun pointed at two other boys who had their hands up and their backs against the alley wall.

If Raoul pulled the trigger, it would be cold-blooded murder.

Silently, Robert got out of his car. He was far enough away that nobody was paying him any attention. The boys with their hands in the air were staring at the gun. Raoul was staring at them.

"Come on, man. We were just kidding around." That was from the tallest boy. The shorter boy said nothing. It looked like he was about to fall down.

"Shut up," Raoul said. "Just shut the hell up."

Damn. He couldn't let Raoul shoot these other kids. His hand inched toward his own gun.

Carmen would hate him. She would never forgive him if he shot her brother.

He edged around his car and took a few steps into the alley. He had his hands in the air, his gun still in his side holster.

"Hey, Raoul," he said softly. "It's Robert. Put your gun down."

Raoul's head swirled toward Robert. "No," he yelled. "I'll kill you, too, if I have to."

"You're not going to kill anybody, Raoul."

"Stay away," Raoul yelled. "Don't come near me."

Robert stopped. "Fine. Just calm down. We can work this out."

"They made me roll around in the garbage like a dog."

Robert could see the boy's shoulders heaving and knew that he was close to breaking down. "They're the animals, then. Not you. Now put your gun away. You don't want to spend the rest of your life paying for this moment, Raoul. It's not worth it."

"They'll get away," Raoul cried. "And tomorrow it will be worse."

"They're not going anywhere. There are about six cops right behind me. The lady who lives upstairs saw everything. She's the one who called it in. Come on, Raoul, you're a good kid. Don't screw up your life."

Chapter Seventeen

The kid didn't put down the gun.

Robert knew he had one last shot. "Don't do this to Carmen, Raoul. Don't let her lose another brother. She won't be able to take it. She's given up everything for you. Don't make her regret it."

Raoul's arms were shaking so badly that Robert was scared the gun was going to go off accidentally.

"I think they might have messed with Carmen's car. They said stuff about her."

Now that got his attention.

"What kind of stuff?" he asked.

"We were just kidding," the taller one said. "We meant no disrespect, man."

Based on that comment, Robert could pretty much figure out what they'd said. That pissed him off. But if they were responsible for Carmen's car, Raoul was going to have to pull him off them.

"Carmen Jimenez's brake lines were cut. I want to know what you know about that." He watched their faces closely and he could tell that he'd surprised them.

"We sprayed the car with paint and JJ broke the window," one of them said. "We didn't do anything with any brake lines. I wouldn't even know how to cut a brake line."

"They might be lying," Raoul yelled.

He didn't think so. "If they're responsible," he said, "then they'll be prosecuted. Trust me on this, Raoul. They won't get away with it. It's not your job to take the law into your own hands."

It took another thirty seconds of painful silence before Raoul lowered his arms. Robert's heart started to beat again when the boy dropped to his knees and laid the gun on the ground. He pointed his finger at the boys. "Stay right where you are," he said. He got close enough to kick Raoul's gun far out of reach. Then he reached out his arm and grabbed the boy and pulled him tight into his body.

"It's going to be okay," Robert said, his voice close to Raoul's ear. "It's all going to be okay."

AN HOUR LATER, Raoul and Robert walked into the apartment. Carmen met them at the door. She wrapped her arms around her brother and held him.

Robert stepped back. He'd called her as soon as he could, but then it had taken another hour to get things straightened out. Beat cops had arrived within minutes of Raoul putting down his weapon. It still made Robert queasy to think how differently things might have turned out if another cop had arrived before he had.

Raoul might have been shot, might have been killed. Carmen might be mourning the loss of another brother.

"I'm sorry," Raoul said, wiping his nose with his sleeve.

"I know, honey. Tell me what happened." She led him over to the couch, where they sat, side by side. Robert took the chair and listened while Raoul told his sister about the bullying that he'd been enduring and how it had all culminated in the alley.

Robert had already heard the explanation once at the police station. Raoul's account of what happened in the alley matched what the eyewitness had called in. The other boys had started it. Raoul had attempted to finish it, once and for all.

"You should have told me," Carmen said, her voice soft.

"I couldn't. I knew you'd want to help but it would only get worse."

Carmen nodded. She was wise to the world of teenagers and probably realized that what he was saying was true.

"Then the stuff with your car happened and I knew they knew where we lived. They had to be stopped."

"I understand," she said. She turned to him. "Any reason to believe that they're responsible for the damage to my car?"

"They admitted to the spray paint and breaking the window. Flatly denied messing with the brakes. I think they were telling the truth. Plus, they were both in school on Monday. Every teacher takes attendance and they didn't miss any classes. I don't think they had an opportunity."

"So they are just a bunch of cowardly bullies," she said.

"Yeah. They won't bother him again," Robert said before she could ask. "I spoke with them and their parents. They're already lawyering up to make a plea bargain on the vandalism charge. I guess they're worried about football scholarships. Anyway, I made it very clear that if one hair on Raoul's head is harmed, that the police are going to be looking in their direction. I think both the kids and their parents got it."

She smiled at him. "Thank you," she whispered. Then she turned back to Raoul.

"Where did you ever get a gun?" Carmen asked.

Robert sat forward in his chair. This was the only part of Raoul's story that hadn't made sense.

"Some guy gave it to me," he said.

"Some guy?" Carmen questioned.

Raoul nodded.

"Some stranger just gave you a gun and you took it?" Carmen asked, her voice heavy with suspicion.

This time Raoul shrugged. "I gave him twenty bucks."

Robert forced himself to keep quiet. The gun had been registered to a Martin Olsen from Oak Park who had reported the gun being stolen from his car over a year ago. There were no prints on it besides Raoul's.

Was it possible that some guy had stolen it and resold it? Sure. Stolen goods got converted into money for drugs every day. It was the banking system that lots of people were familiar with.

But something just didn't seem right. And Raoul had not copped to being involved with the shooting at Speedy's Used Cars even though Robert had once again asked him about it.

Robert had called in a few favors with the state's attorney's office, and Raoul would not be prosecuted for possessing the stolen gun. JJ's and Beau's parents, likely wanting similar leniency for their sons, hadn't pushed in the opposite direction.

"I'm sorry, Carmen," Raoul said. "I never meant to worry you. Can I go to my room now?"

Carmen kissed his cheek and nodded. "We'll eat something in a little bit," she said.

Robert looked at the clock on the wall. Half past six. He'd left Sawyer a little more than two hours earlier.

He waited until he heard Raoul's door close. "I'd like to stay but I have to go," he said.

"Of course. Robert, I don't know how to thank you. I don't know exactly what happened in that alley but what I think is that I have my brother because of you."

He shook his head. "I didn't do that much. He really didn't want to kill those boys. He'd just boxed himself into a corner."

Carmen's eyes filled with tears. "A gun. In my wildest dreams, I'd never have considered that he'd have a gun. I'd like to get my hands on that person," she added.

"Nobody forced him to buy it," Robert said, keeping his tone neutral.

She frowned at him, then shook her head. "You're right. The responsibility lies with him. I know I'm too quick to cut him some slack. It's just that when I think of how close I came to losing him, I just can't stand it."

He wanted to tell her his suspicions about Speedy's Used Cars but he just couldn't. Not tonight. She'd been through enough. Robert reached for her hand. "It's over. Forget it."

"No. I need to say something. I lost one brother and today, I almost lost another one. I would have. Whether he'd killed those boys or they'd killed him. Either way, I'd have lost him."

"He's lucky to have you. In lots of families, this

would have caused a huge blowout. But you listened. You gave him a chance to explain."

She sighed. "I wanted him to know that he could tell me anything. You know, it's a terrible burden to have to hide things from those who love you. I know, better than most."

Was she hiding something from him? Robert rubbed his chin. "I'm not sure I understand."

Carmen got up and started to pace around the room. "I made a mistake when I was not much older than Raoul. A big mistake."

She looked miserable. "Honey, that's in the past. You don't need to tell me."

She stopped. "I have to tell someone. I have to. It's killing me."

She was scaring him. "Okay. I'm listening. Please, just sit down. Talk to me."

She sat in the chair across from him. "My junior year of high school, I fell in love with a boy who loved football more than he loved me. When I got pregnant, all he could see was his hopes and dreams ending. He didn't want me or the baby."

The bastard. "What happened?"

"I couldn't tell my parents. I just couldn't. They'd worked so hard. Hector had already split off from the family, had gone his own way with the gang. That had almost killed them. I couldn't disappoint them again." She clasped her hands together. "My mother barely spoke English and my father worked at a minimum wage job. But still, they had dreams that their children would have a better life."

"What happened?"

"I hid my pregnancy. And every day, I tried to do something so that I'd lose the baby. I jumped off chairs. I turned cartwheels in gym class. I ran miles on the track at school. And eleven weeks into my pregnancy, my wish came true. I miscarried. I never told anybody."

His heart broke for the young girl she'd been. "I'm sorry there was nobody there for you," he said.

"It was almost exactly thirteen years ago. On January 18."

Robert did the calculation and realized that the day he'd knocked on Carmen's door, the day she'd been crying, had been the eighteenth. "You were just a kid, Carmen. A kid faced with an adult circumstance. And everything you did probably had nothing to do with you losing the baby. It probably just happened."

"I guess we'll never know. And that haunts me. I was a kid trying to handle an adult situation. Raoul had to make an adult decision today. I'm just thankful to you that he didn't have to do it on his own."

Neither of them would ever have to be on their own if he had his way. But now wasn't the time to tell her that.

"What I've learned over the years is that none of us can go back," Carmen continued. "Raoul can't go back to being the kid he was before he threatened to kill two boys. He can't go back. A person can only go forward. Thanks to you, he's got a future to look forward to."

She stood up. "I have a future to look forward to," she added. "Now maybe you understand a little better why I waited thirteen years to be with another man. In some sick way, I was punishing myself, repentance for my sins, if you will. I had done something very wrong. I denied myself pleasure or love because I didn't think I deserved it."

He felt his soul rip for the youth she'd lost. "You so deserve it," he said.

She rubbed the back of her hand across his cheek. "I know. It's amazing. I know it now. You helped me see it."

He wished he didn't have to go. But now that they had a lead on the serial killer, everybody would work all night if necessary. He stood up and put his coat on. "I'm sorry, but I really do have to go. I'm needed back at work. I want to talk to you about something but now isn't the right time. I just can't do it right now."

"I understand," she said and wrapped her arms around his neck. She pulled his face toward her and soundly kissed him.

And he let himself drink in all the goodness that was Carmen Jimenez.

When they stopped kissing, he rested his forehead against hers. "Now I really wish I didn't have to go to work."

"We could go out in the hallway and make out again," she said, humor in her tone.

"Don't tempt me," he said. He lifted his head. "I don't want to put a damper on things but you know, we still don't know who messed with your brakes. You and Raoul need to continue to be vigilant about your safety."

"We will. We aren't going anywhere tonight. No need to worry about us. Mrs. Minelli is taking Raoul to school. I'll catch a cab to work."

He kissed her again. "Okay. Good night."

BY THE TIME Robert caught up with Sawyer, he'd interviewed Barry Taylor and two other staff members who lived in the same general vicinity. "What do you think?" Robert asked.

"I think Mr. Willow was right," Sawyer said. "Barry Taylor is an odd duck. Well, he was more right than you might imagine."

"I don't get it."

"We got his permission to look around his house, and I think maybe the only thing he takes vengeance on *is* ducks. He carves them, paints them, mosaic-tiles them, you get the picture. Every room of his house, there are ducks. The artwork in his house, all ducks."

"So maybe that's why he didn't play well with the other instructors? They were human?"

Sawyer smiled. "It's a possibility. I have to admit, when I saw the carving tools, I got a little excited, given that our guy likes to take home body parts for trophies. That's why I asked permission to search. The guy didn't even hesitate."

"Could he be doing the killing somewhere else?"

"Of course. But here's the kicker. He doesn't have a car. He said he didn't, that he didn't even have a driver's license. I was able to verify that with the State. I also took the time to talk to a few of his neighbors after I left, and they have never seen him in a car. He rides his bike everywhere."

"Our guy has a car or use of a car," Robert said, shaking his head. "He's spreading bodies out all over the city. Not doing that on a bike."

"I think we can scratch odd guy number one off the list. Anyway, the other two staff members that I spoke to seemed pretty normal. One has a teenage boy and I could tell the killings had been especially upsetting for him. The other had been traveling recently and was happy to show us his passport, which verified that he wasn't even in the country when the killings started. What was interesting was that when I asked both of them if there was somebody on staff who had stood out as odd or different, they both said Douglass Sparrow. That he was a real loner."

"Maybe he was afraid that Barry Taylor was going to start carving him. You know, ducks today, sparrows tomorrow," Robert suggested.

Sawyer rolled his eyes. "Keep your day job," he said. "Come on. Let's go. It's going to be a long night."

DOUGLASS SPARROW LIVED three blocks from where victim number three had been found. That didn't necessarily mean anything since all the other victims had been found miles away.

They knocked on the door of the small brick home and waited. They both had flashlights out and on. It had been dark for hours, and Sparrow evidently didn't believe in porch lights. The temperature had once again dropped and was now hovering around zero.

"I'm going to go check the back," Robert said. He walked between the houses, which had been built so damn close together that if neighbors both leaned out their windows, they could pass the proverbial cup of sugar.

The back door was locked. Robert pounded on the door and waited a couple minutes. The night was quiet otherwise and he didn't hear or see anything that gave him any indication that somebody was home.

Maybe Sparrow was at the grocery store or a movie?

Or maybe he was scouting for his next victim?

Robert circled back to Sawyer. "Let's talk to some neighbors."

The neighbor on the right was a woman in her sixties. In her living room, there was an ironing board and a treadmill, both set up in front of the flat-screen television. She was obviously a multitasker.

They did introductions. Olivia Borsk was her name, and she was a widow.

When they asked about Douglass Sparrow, she looked satisfied. It wasn't the reaction they'd expected.

"It's about time you got here," she said.

"Time?" Robert asked.

"I've called three times. That's twice more than I should have needed to."

"What did you call about, Mrs. Borsk?" Sawyer asked.

"His sidewalk, for goodness' sake. He never shovels it. Only house between here and the grocery store that doesn't do what he's supposed to. Forces me to walk out into the street and that's wrong."

Robert and Sawyer shared a look. "Have you ever spoken to Mr. Sparrow about your concerns?"

The woman huffed. "Two *s*s and two *r*s."

"What?" Sawyer asked.

"Douglass Sparrow. Two *s*s and two *r*s. When he introduces himself, that's what he says to everybody. Pompous ass."

"Does Mr. Sparrow have much company?" Robert asked.

"No. But then again, he's rarely here."

"What do you mean?" Robert asked.

"What I mean is that the man is only here about half the time. I know because his car is old and loud and I have to turn up my television to hear the news when he pulls up. Maybe if he was here more often, he could do the sidewalk. Or maybe, if you people talked to him, he would do the sidewalk."

You people. Robert could not look at Sawyer. Otherwise, he would bust a gut and the woman would have a whole other reason to be calling the police department.

"Yes, of course," Robert said. "What kind of car does Mr. Sparrow drive?"

"Black and noisy. Two doors. Mildred and Ben, his folks, bought it for him when he was in high school."

"Does Mr. Sparrow work out of town? Is that why he's gone?" Sawyer asked.

The woman shook her head. "I don't even think he works. He inherited this house from his parents last year. The Sparrows died in a car accident, poor things. At least they went together. Anyway, they were always saying that he was going to be a famous musician someday. I felt sorry for them. They couldn't even see the fact that their son was as odd as a three-dollar bill."

"You don't think he's been successful as a musician?"

The woman shrugged. "He was bagging groceries at the supermarket down the street up until his parents' deaths. That doesn't seem all that successful to me."

Robert stood up. "Thank you. You've been very helpful."

They were halfway out the door when Mrs. Borsk called after them. "What about the sidewalk?"

"If we see Mr. Sparrow, we'll make sure we mention it," said Robert.

Once they were back in the car, Sawyer rubbed his hands together. "I think this could be our guy. The music fits. And lots of times, something sets these idiots off. Maybe that was his parents' deaths? Maybe there wasn't anybody left who believed in him? The only thing I don't get is that he's rarely home. Where the hell do you think he is?"

Robert shook his head as he pulled away from the curb. "That's the weird part. Let's figure out what he's driving," he said. He picked up his cell phone and when the call was answered, he gave them the pertinent details.

"I need information on a car owned by either Douglass Sparrow or Mildred or Ben Sparrow." He rattled off the home address and hung up.

It didn't take long for him to get a return call. Robert listened and nodded. "Okay, thanks. Put out a BOLO for that vehicle with instructions to not apprehend or approach. I just want to know where it is."

Robert turned to Sawyer. "Black Mercury Cougar, 1995."

Chapter Eighteen

They got a judge to order a search warrant for Douglass Sparrow's home.

It didn't take long to search. There was lots of old furniture that his parents had probably had for years. He had a few clothes in the closet and dresser drawers. Some toiletries in the bathroom and a jar each of mustard and pickle relish in his refrigerator.

"Sparrow must eat out all the time," Robert said. He opened cupboards and found a few plates and two cups.

Sawyer stood in the middle of the kitchen with his hands on his hips. "It's almost as if…"

"He doesn't really live here," Robert said, finishing the sentence. "Which matches what Mrs. Borsk said that he's hardly ever around."

"So why do you keep a house but you don't live in it?" Sawyer asked.

"Because where you're really living is a secret," Robert said.

"Gay?" Sawyer asked.

Robert shook his head. "Parents both dead. No high-profile job. Little risk if the secret gets out."

"Into something illegal?" was Sawyer's next guess.

Robert met his partner's eyes. "Like luring young boys to your place and then killing them?"

"Bingo," Sawyer said.

Robert rubbed his hand across his face. They were running out of time. "We need this guy's bank account. Maybe he's writing out rent checks. And his IRS records, too. Maybe there are earnings from another employer."

"It's late," Sawyer said.

"Looks as if we're going to have to get a few people out of bed," Robert answered, already pulling out his phone.

WHEN CARMEN GOT up on Wednesday morning, she carefully opened Raoul's bedroom door. He was still asleep. Had pushed off his covers at some point and he lay sprawled in the single bed, dressed in an old T-shirt and sweats.

He looked very young and vulnerable.

And he'd threatened to kill two people yesterday.

The two images were so jarringly different that it still made her head hurt.

Thank God Robert had been there. In his calm way, he'd been able to intervene and he had saved lives. He'd certainly given Raoul his life back.

Robert had wanted to ask her something but had said that he'd wait for a better time. What the heck?

Maybe he wanted her to go away with him? That day after the movie they'd had that ridiculous conversation about tropical vacations. Aruba? Bermuda? The Cayman Islands?

If he asked, would she go?

Could she leave Raoul?

Two weeks ago, she'd have said no. But now, she'd had a taste of living, a taste of feeling whole as she shattered in a man's arms.

She'd had a taste of loving Robert. So if he asked, she'd make sure that Raoul was in Liz and Sawyer's capable hands and she'd go.

She opened a cupboard and pulled coffee out. Got a pot started and walked back to the bathroom for her shower. By the time she'd finished and dried her hair, she could hear Raoul moving around in the apartment.

She got dressed, pulled her hair back into a low ponytail and put on a little makeup. She'd just finished with mascara when her phone rang.

It was Robert. She smiled at herself in the mirror. "Hi," she said.

"Good morning," he said. "I just wanted to check in and make sure everything was okay."

She'd been taking care of herself and Raoul for a long time. Had been pretty proud of that fact. Was it wrong that it felt so good to finally have someone who cared about them, maybe even worried about them? "We're fine," she said. "Uneventful night. Mrs. Minelli should be here any minute."

"Look, I wish I knew what the day was going to bring. Maybe we could catch a late dinner together?"

He sounded wistful. And tired. "Did you work late?" she asked.

"All night," he admitted. "I caught a catnap this morning in my chair."

"Oh, Robert." If anyone thought police work was glamorous, they didn't understand it.

"We're getting close," he said. "Can't say much more than that but I think we're on the right track."

"Good luck," she said.

"Just be careful today, Carmen. Frank Sage is a wild card. We can't prove that he messed with your brakes but my gut tells me that he's a bad guy. I've got somebody keeping an eye on him, and he's already been to his coffee shop and he's on his way to work. I think you'll be okay."

She felt very warm inside. Robert Hanson was watching out for her.

"Call me later," she said. "Even if it's really late."

She heard his breath catch and it made her feel pretty powerful. "I will."

By the time she got to the kitchen, Raoul was at the table with a bowl of cereal in front of him.

But he wasn't eating. He was just staring at his hands, which were cupped around his bowl.

"Morning," she said. She poured herself a cup of coffee.

"Morning," he answered.

He looked tired, and she suspected that he hadn't slept well. Was he worried about school? About the two boys who were no doubt going to be there that morning?

"I don't think those boys will bother you," she said. "Remember what Robert said?"

Raoul nodded. "I'm not worried about that."

But he was clearly worried about something. She sat down at the table and sipped her coffee. After about two minutes, Raoul looked up from his cupped hands.

"I wasn't honest with you last night," he said. "You were great about everything and I couldn't even tell you the truth."

Her heart sped up. There was more?

"Then maybe you better take another stab at it," she said, hoping that she sounded more confident than she was.

He looked her in the eyes. "I didn't pay somebody twenty dollars for the gun," he said. "Someone gave it to me."

"Who?"

"This guy. He's about your age, I guess. He says his name is Apollo. He was a friend of Hector's."

Hector's. She felt her heart start to beat even faster. All of Hector's friends had been bad news. She'd known many of them because he was just two years older. She'd never heard of anyone named Apollo.

"How long have you known this man?"

"Not long. He said that Hector had asked him to watch out for me. He wanted me to have Hector's gun."

Hector had had a gun. She'd seen it in the waistband of his shorts just days before he'd died. The people he hung with all had guns. But Hector's had been recovered from his body, confiscated by the police.

Was it possible that he'd had another gun?

Perhaps. But after all these years for it to surface with some lame story about Hector asking for his baby brother to be watched over seemed preposterous.

No way.

"Apollo said that he met you a couple times. He knew your name."

He was going to know more than her name by the time she got through with him. What kind of trash gave a gun to a fifteen-year-old?

"There's something else," he said. He looked even more miserable. "You're going to be so mad at me."

He was scaring her. "I may be angry," she admitted. "But you need to tell me everything or I can't help."

"The other night, I used the gun to shoot out some windshields at a used car place. Speedy's. I'm not exactly sure how many cars."

Her heart sank. Shooting out car windows.

He'd committed a crime. Her brother was a criminal. "When? How?"

"On Sunday night. I snuck out while you and Alexa were busy in the kitchen. I met Apollo there. He wanted to teach me how to shoot."

She was going to rip this guy's head off.

"We're going to have to tell the police," she said. The idea of Raoul having a police record made her want to throw up, but they had to do what was right.

"I think they know," Raoul said, tears in his eyes. "At least I think Robert does."

What? How could that be? "Why would you think that?"

"He's asked me about it a couple times."

Robert had reason to believe that her brother had a gun and had used that gun to commit a crime and yet he'd said nothing. She felt sick and hollow and terribly betrayed.

He knew that Raoul was her life.

She was such an idiot. She'd gotten blinded by the attention and she'd lost track of what was important.

Raoul. He was important. And he'd gotten himself into a bunch of trouble.

And now he needed her help.

"Do you know how to contact Apollo?" she asked.

"I'm supposed to meet him at eight o'clock this morning, outside my school."

"I'm going with you," she said. She got up and carefully pushed her chair in. Her bones felt very brittle. "I don't believe that he was a friend of Hector's. He certainly wasn't looking out for you when he gave you a gun so that you could vandalize someone's property. What you did was wrong," she said.

"I know. It's all I can think about. I'm so sorry, Carmen."

She could forgive Raoul. He was a teenager who had gotten caught up in something that was bigger than him. It was harder to forgive Robert. He was an adult and he hadn't been honest with her.

"What about Mrs. Minelli?" Raoul asked. "She's driving this morning."

"I'll call her," Carmen said. "I'll let her know that I'm taking you to school. Once I tell Apollo that he is never to contact you again, then we're going to the police. You're going to tell them everything. There's going to be consequences to your actions, Raoul. You understand that, don't you?"

He nodded. "I just want this to be over with."

"Me, too," she said. "Finish getting ready," she added, as she walked back to her bedroom. Once inside the door, she pressed her hands to her eyes.

She would not cry. She would not.

She and Raoul would get through this.

The same way they'd gotten through everything else. Together.

She picked up her cell phone, which she always kept on her nightstand during the night. She punched in Robert's number. She was relieved when it went right to voice mail.

"It's Carmen," she said. "You…you should have told me, Robert. You should have told me about Speedy's and your suspicions about Raoul. I deserved to know that my brother had a gun. I deserved the truth from you." She took a big breath. "Don't call me again."

WHEN THE CAB pulled to the corner, Carmen tossed a ten at the driver and opened her door. The cab had been late picking them up, plus they'd hit some slow traffic. She'd been impatient to get here, to meet the man who claimed to be Hector's friend who had lured her fifteen-year-old brother into being a criminal.

She wrapped her scarf tight around her neck. Raoul slid out of the cab and slammed the door shut. "Do you see him?" Carmen asked. The sidewalk was heavy with human traffic, people all bundled up, walking with their heads down to avoid the wind.

She looked at her watch. Seven minutes after eight. He should be here.

For the first time, Carmen got nervous. It was broad daylight and there were lots of people around but still her gut was telling her that something was wrong. She heard Raoul's cell phone buzz. He pulled it out. It was a text.

"It's him," he said.

"He has your cell phone number?" she asked. Then she waved her hand. "Never mind. That's not important. What does it say?"

"Be there soon."

They weren't waiting. They were going to the police and telling them everything. Then they could find Apollo and deal with him. "Come on," she said. "Let's go."

Damn, she wished she had her car. There were no cabs. She walked toward Mahoney High, feeling that she'd be safe there.

They'd walked less than thirty feet before a man emerged from the bushes that lined the street. He fell into step next to them. They were three abreast on the wide sidewalk, her, then Raoul, then the man. She pulled on Raoul's sleeve, wanting to get him away from the man.

"Not so fast, pretty sister," he said.

She stopped and looked at the man. He had dark hair pulled back into a ponytail. His skin was very pale. She did not recognize him. If he'd been a friend of Hector's, he was one that she'd never met.

He was probably five-eight and a hundred and sixty pounds. Not an overly big guy. But she realized that didn't matter when she saw that he had a very deadly looking gun in his hand and it was pointed at Raoul.

"We want nothing to do with you," she said, hating that her voice was shaking. "You just go your way and we'll go ours and we'll forget that we ever saw each other."

"And spoil the fun?" he asked. "I don't think so. You're an unexpected complication but certainly not one that I can't deal with." He motioned with his index finger. "Step through the bushes. There's a black car. Get in the driver's side. If you make one wrong move, you're going to have another dead brother."

It was crazy. There were people on the sidewalks, on both sides of the street. Mostly kids. Some adults. But nobody was paying attention to them. They were just hurrying to school or to work.

She looked in the man's eyes. They were completely devoid of emotion. She wanted to refuse, to tell him to go to hell.

Raoul could be dead before she finished her sentence.

She turned and started walking, and she could hear Raoul and the man behind her.

Chapter Nineteen

With the exception of the short nap, Robert had been awake for more than thirty hours. They had pored through Sparrow's banking records. He had over two hundred thousand dollars in the bank. It had all come from one deposit that occurred about thirty days after his parents' deaths.

Life insurance proceeds, most likely.

He wrote out a few checks, for utilities and property taxes, for the property they had searched. Each month he also withdrew a thousand dollars in cash. Maybe he spent that on gas and food and all the other things that ate up dollars, but there was no way to know.

During the night, teams of detectives had spoken to every one of Douglass Sparrow's former coworkers and his neighbors, trying to glean any kernel of information. That hadn't made them very popular. And in normal circumstances, they would have never woken people up in the middle of the night to ask questions.

But these were not normal circumstances.

They were waiting to hear that another dead boy had been found.

"We need to start on the students," Sawyer said.

There were over four hundred names on the list. It was like looking for a needle in a haystack. "We need to separate the boys from the girls."

Tasha, three desks away, held up a sheet of paper. "Done."

Robert smiled. "You need a raise."

"Got that right. One hundred and ninety boys. Sorted alphabetically."

Robert scanned the list. About halfway down, a name jumped off the page.

Raoul Jimenez.

Holy hell.

He needed to call Carmen, tell her what was going on. He picked up his phone, which was charging on his desk. He saw that he had a voice mail message and realized that his phone was on vibrate.

He listened to the message.

And his heart sank.

I deserved to know that my brother had a gun. I deserved the truth from you.

He'd talked to her just thirty minutes earlier. Everything had been fine. Now she was so angry her words were clipped. *Don't call me again.*

That wasn't going to happen. He punched in her

number. It rang four times before it went to voice mail. "Carmen, it's Robert. I got your message. Listen, I don't know what happened but we need to talk. Before you or Raoul do anything, you need to call me. Please." He hung up.

He dialed Carmen's office phone and left a similar message.

By now, Sawyer had scanned the list, seen Raoul's name, and was dialing Liz's number. From the side of the conversation that Robert could hear, he knew that Liz had not yet seen Carmen.

Both last night and this morning, Carmen had said that Raoul was getting a ride to school with Jacob's mother. He had that kid's phone number. Carmen had given it to him.

He scrolled through his phone and pushed the number. It rang three times before it was answered.

"Hello."

"Is this Jacob Minelli?"

"Yeah."

"My name is Detective Robert Hanson. I'm a friend of Carmen and Raoul Jimenez. Is Raoul with you?"

"No. Why would he be?"

"Your mother drove you both to school."

"Nope. Carmen called this morning and said that she was taking Raoul to school. I've got to go. Class starts in a minute and if you get caught with a phone, they take it away from you."

Robert hung up and shoved back his desk chair. He started running for the door. He stopped halfway through the station and yelled back at Tasha. "Every car in the vicinity of Mahoney High needs to be on the lookout for a woman, Hispanic, five-three, a hundred and ten pounds, likely wearing a blue cape. Also, a Hispanic fifteen-year-old boy, five feet, ninety pounds, likely wearing a red jacket."

"You want them picked up?" Tasha asked.

"Hell, yes." He wanted them safe, in his arms.

CARMEN GRIPPED THE steering wheel of the old car, unwilling to let the man see that she was shaking. He'd made Raoul climb in back and he sat in front, twisted in his seat, his gun aimed at Raoul.

Carmen didn't intend for them to be in the car long. The first cop she saw, she was going to run into the squad car. Hard enough that the guy would get spooked and run but not so hard that either she or Raoul were seriously hurt.

"Turn here," he said.

They'd gone less than two blocks. She didn't have a choice. She turned.

Halfway down the alley, he motioned for her to make a quick right. She did and found herself in a small space, just big enough for the car. It looked as if many years ago it had been a small courtyard. There were scraggly, bare branches curving upward on the brick walls. She could see patches of dirt underneath the mostly snow-covered ground.

There was a back door on the bottom level. Above it, there was a sign. Augusta Custom Framing. It didn't look as if anybody had used the back door in some time.

There was a set of wooden stairs that rose from the ground up to the second level. He pointed at them. "Let's go."

She waited for Raoul to get out of the car. She grabbed his hand and squeezed it.

"Sweet," said the man. Then he pushed her forward.

At the top of the landing, he handed her a key and made her unlock the door. It opened into a kitchen that had an old tile floor, a small sink and an avocado-green stove. It smelled like bacon and she could see a dirty plate in the sink that was smeared with egg yolk.

The bastard had had breakfast before he'd come to the school. That, more than anything that had happened so far, told her that they were dealing with someone who had no conscience.

"In there," he said.

She walked into the living room. There was a couch and one chair. There was a table in the corner.

On it was a stack of red handkerchiefs.

And she remembered the conversation that night

at Liz and Sawyer's house. *The victims have all been found with red handkerchiefs in their mouths. Shows an arrogance on his part—that he's so confident that he won't be caught that he can afford to leave clues at the scene.*

She looked at her brother. He looked scared to death. *Oh, Raoul, what have we done?*

THERE WAS NO sign of Carmen or Raoul. He hadn't really expected to see any. School had already started. If they were on time, the cab would have already dropped Raoul off and Carmen would be on her way to work.

Robert tried her cell phone again. It went straight to voice mail. He didn't leave one.

Answer your damn phone, Carmen.

He parked in a no-parking zone and pushed the buzzer on the school door. It felt as if it had been a lifetime since he'd been at the school but it was really just forty-eight hours ago. Then he'd been here to bust Raoul's chops about Speedy's Used Cars. Now, he just wanted to hug the kid and celebrate that he and his sister were okay.

But he wasn't going to get that chance, he realized, when the school secretary confirmed that Raoul's homeroom teacher had already reported him as absent from class.

Now what?

Robert walked out of the office and leaned against the gray metal lockers. Now what?

He looked up. Three boys were walking down the hall. One was looking at his phone, and the other one was laughing at something his friend was saying.

Friend.

What was it that Carmen had said? Jacob Minelli and Raoul had been best friends since third grade.

Robert strode back into the office. "I need to see Jacob Minelli. Right now."

The woman didn't hesitate. "I'll have to look up his first period," she said. She typed a few letters into her computer. Then she pressed a button. "Mrs. Black, can you please send Jacob Minelli to the office."

"Yes," came the static-filled response.

Robert waited impatiently, watching out the windows of the office. He saw a kid come down the steps at the far end of the hallway and recognized him from the photos in Carmen's apartment.

He met him halfway.

"I'm Detective Robert Hanson," he said.

"Are you still looking for Raoul?" the kid asked.

Robert nodded. "Neither Carmen nor Raoul are answering their phones. Raoul never made it to school."

"Look, I'd like to help but Raoul and I are sort of

not talking to one another right now. I don't think he's going to call me."

That didn't match what Carmen had said. "Why?"

The kid didn't say anything.

"Listen, Jacob. Raoul may in trouble. Carmen, too. I need the truth and I need it now."

"He's been doing some crazy stuff lately."

"Like what?"

"Like carrying a gun. He showed it to me."

"Did he tell you where he got the gun?" Robert asked.

Jacob nodded. "Some guy named Apollo gave it to him. What kind of name is that?"

Apollo. The God of Music.

Robert pressed a hand against his stomach. His coffee was about to make a return appearance. "Did you ever meet Apollo?"

The kid shook his head.

Robert wanted to slam his fist into the locker. "Okay, thanks," he said.

Jacob stared at him. "I may have seen his car," he said. "I had a birthday party. And Raoul got mad and left before everybody else. I saw him going and ran out to stop him. He's been my best friend for a long time and I didn't want to fight with him. He was about a block ahead of me when I saw a car pull up and offer him a ride."

"What kind of car?"

"An old black one like my uncle used to drive."

"You get a license plate?" Robert asked, hoping like hell his luck was about to change.

The kid shook his head.

"Make or model?" Robert asked.

"I'm pretty sure it was an old Mercury Cougar. They have a real distinct style."

ROBERT'S HANDS WERE shaking when he pulled out his cell phone and punched up his boss. When Lieutenant Fischer answered, Robert didn't waste any time.

"I need all the street camera video from around Mahoney High School this morning. We're looking for Douglass Sparrow's black Mercury Cougar and—" Robert stopped and drew in a deep breath "—I think it's possible that he has Raoul and Carmen Jimenez."

Lieutenant Fischer was silent for a long minute. Then he asked, "Are you okay?"

Hell, no. He was a wreck. So scared that his mind seemed to have stopped working.

"Don't worry about me," he said.

"Be careful," his boss said. "Keep your head in the game."

His head, his heart. Everything was in the game. Because Carmen was everything, meant everything.

She'd sounded so angry.

He'd been wrong to hide his suspicions from

her. Realized that now. Maybe that whole horrible scene in the alley with Raoul and those two boys would have never happened if he'd been more forthcoming.

No wonder she didn't want him to call her again.

The diamond ring felt heavy in his pocket. What the hell had he done?

"Have you talked to Sawyer?" Robert asked.

"Just got off the phone with him. He tracked down a former coworker of Sparrow's from his grocery store bagging days. Said that the guy was always talking about going to some fancy music school and that he was going to be famous someday."

But something had derailed those plans and he'd found himself bagging groceries and teaching music in the summer to a bunch of sweaty middle-schoolers.

And somewhere along the way, he'd decided to start killing them.

"Who are you?" Carmen asked.

"Didn't Raoul tell you? I'm Apollo."

"You weren't a friend of Hector's," she accused.

The man smiled. He was sprawled in the chair, his butt halfway down, his legs extended. She'd have thought he was relaxed if he didn't have the gun pointed straight at Raoul.

"Ah, so he did tell you about me." The man

looked satisfied. "Brilliant, don't you think? The internet makes everything so easy. Birth records, death records, addresses. After I met Raoul at band camp last year, it was easy to find out more about the Jimenez family. Hector's stabbing didn't make front-page news of the paper but there was a nice little article in the archives."

She remembered that article. Remembered how her mother had carefully cut it out and put it in the Bible that she kept on her nightstand. And Carmen suspected that every night until her mother died just two years later, the woman had prayed over it.

It made her furious to think that this man had used it to target Raoul, to make him think that he was somehow closer to the brother that he'd never had the chance to know.

"You bastard," she said. "You won't get away with this."

He laughed. "Of course I will. It's perfect. The police will never find me here. There's no record of me here. I give the man who owns the frame shop cash every month. He's happy because his wife doesn't know he has the money and I'm happy because everything is in his name. I don't exist."

"The police know more than what was reported in the paper. They're very close."

The corner of his mouth raised up in a sneer. "I'm not the bad person here," he said. "I'm saving them. From a lifetime of disappointment. From a lifetime of never realizing the dream. Because the dream is an illusion. A damn illusion."

He stood up and started pacing around the room. "They fill your head with all kinds of lies. And you start making plans. And then one day, they say, ha-ha, we were only kidding. You're not that talented. You're nothing."

He took two big steps toward her, leaned into her face, and yelled. "I am not nothing."

"Of course you aren't," she said. She needed to calm him down. "What instrument did you play?"

He cocked his head. "The piano, the oboe, the drums. The music just came to me. I heard it in my sleep."

"I bet you were very good," she said.

"My parents were proud of me," he said, sounding like a little boy. "But then they gave up, too. Said that I needed to do something with my life. That was wrong of them. You should never give up on your child."

She didn't know what to say to that. It didn't seem to matter because he was on a roll.

He smiled at her. "You know they died in a car accident. Their brakes failed, just like yours. But you didn't die. That was really too bad."

She heard Raoul's gasp but she didn't look at him. "So you tampered with my brakes. Why?"

"It was Raoul's fault. He was pulling away. He was going to choose you over me. I couldn't have that. I'd worked too hard on him. He was tougher than the other boys."

She licked her lips.

"Do you want to hear about them?" he asked.

She needed to buy time. To figure a way out of this mess. "Yes. Yes, I would."

Raoul was looking at her as if she were crazy.

Apollo smiled. "Johnnie Whitmore was the first one. Actually, I thought he would be the only one. But then it was so nice that I had to do it again."

She was going to throw up. Swallowing hard, she nodded, as if she was really interested in what he was saying.

"Johnnie wasn't very respectful to me. I was his teacher. The expert. He was lucky to have me at that crappy little camp. You know, he was the only one of the boys who remembered me. Of course, my hair was different and I didn't have these contact lenses then. But he knew me right away. I told him that I was making a CD. He wanted to be part of that. Suddenly, I had value."

She risked a glance at Raoul. He hadn't known about the red handkerchiefs, but he'd figured out who Apollo was. She could see it on his face. She wanted to reach out to assure him that she was going to get them out of there.

"But you decided to do it again?" she said.

He nodded. "Ben Johanson was the easiest of them all. I told him that I was his father. I told him that I had always loved his mother and that once I got to know him a little better, I was going to be back in his mother's life, in his life. The poor kid just wanted a dad. He hung out here several times before it had to end."

"Of course," Carmen said.

"Gabe Monroe needed to be taught a lesson. He had no respect for the music. He came to camp like he had a right to be there. I saw him sitting behind his sister's drums, bragging that he was going to be at band camp the next year. He had no idea the work that it takes, no idea of the sacrifice a musician makes. Let's just say he had stopped boasting by the time I finished him off."

Carmen glanced at her watch. It had been almost twenty minutes since Apollo had stepped out of the bushes.

"Henry Wright was almost as gullible as Ben Johanson. On the camp enrollment sheet, there was a question about musical aspirations. Henry had answered that he wanted to go to Stalwart Academy. I never forgot that because I, too, wanted to go to Stalwart. Once he believed I was trying to recruit him, he was more than willing to visit my home. I don't think he was very impressed, however." He motioned with his hand, as if he were showing off a prize property. "I guess we'll never know, will we?"

"I guess not," she said.

Apollo walked over and put his hand on Raoul's head. Raoul flinched and it took everything Carmen had to stay in her chair. "You haven't asked why I picked Raoul."

Could she bear this? "Why?"

"Because he reminds me of myself. He works hard, does all the right things. It won't be enough. Just like it wasn't enough for me. And of course, I've already told you how I got to know him. It was my most brilliant effort to date."

"If Raoul reminds you of yourself then you must care about him. You can still let us go. It's not too late for you to do the right thing."

He stood up. "I am doing the right thing," he yelled. Then he grabbed her arm and pulled her up from the couch.

FROM THE TRAFFIC command center, they fed images from the street surveillance cameras into the computer screen in his car. Lieutenant Fischer was back at the station watching the same images. Sawyer was en route to join Robert.

The blocks near Mahoney High were highly traveled business districts. Fortunately, with the fresh snow, traffic was light and moving slower than usual. In this particular area, they had cameras at every intersection. So, while there were portions of the street where activity could not be viewed, they could easily track movement in and out of the area.

Because they had the approximate time and location, it took them just minutes to find the car. A black '95 Mercury Cougar. It cruised through one intersection but not the next. There were no side streets between the two intersections.

"He parked somewhere in this area," Robert said, pointing to the map on the side of his screen. "Keep the tape going," he said.

They kept watching, fast-forwarding when they could. "Stop," Robert said. "I think that's him. Get closer," he said.

The technician running the tape zoomed in.

Oh, no. Robert was grateful he was sitting or his legs might have given out. The camera angle was good and they could see Carmen driving. She looked terrified. Apollo was sitting next to her, half-turned in his seat.

They could not see Raoul in the backseat but Robert was confident that he was there.

They tracked the car through the next two intersections. The equipment was sophisticated enough that they could calculate that Carmen was driving twenty-eight miles per hour.

Then suddenly, the car disappeared.

Robert put his finger on the screen. "I'm less than a block from there."

"Wait for backup," Lieutenant Fischer instructed. Like hell. Robert started driving.

When he saw the alley, he knew that was where they had disappeared to. He drove down, stopping when he saw the black car pulled into the small area that might once have been a delivery area but now was home to garbage containers and just enough space for one car.

He got out of his car. He took off his winter coat and replaced it with a bulletproof vest. Street level, there was a back door to a custom framing shop. There were no tracks leading up to it. The steep steps up to the second floor were a different story. Several people had walked them.

He clicked on his radio, gave the dispatcher his position and said, "I'm going in." He clicked off before anyone could tell him not to.

He put his hand in his pocket and touched the ring case. It felt warm and solid. He took that as a good sign.

He started up the steps and was at the landing when he heard Carmen scream.

He kicked the door open and went in low.

Apollo was across the room, a knife in one hand, a gun in the other. Raoul had his hands spread on the coffee table. He was crying. Carmen, tied to a chair, watched in terror.

"Police," he yelled. "Put down your—"

The bullet hit him in the shoulder, knocking him back. Searing, white-hot pain spread through his arm. He stayed upright and returned fire. Three shots.

And he saw the man go down.

Raoul ran to his sister. They were both alive.

"Robert?" Carmen said.

"I'm going to be okay," he said, right before he blacked out.

ROBERT WOKE UP in a hospital bed. His arm hurt like hell and he felt sick to his stomach. He tried to move but stopped quickly when pain rocketed through him.

"Good afternoon, Mr. Hanson." A young man dressed in dark blue scrubs was five feet away, his fingers clicking on a keyboard. "I'm Keith, your nurse. How do you feel?"

"Where's Carmen?" he asked. His throat was so dry.

The young man smiled. "You have some visitors outside. You can see them in a few minutes. You were shot. Do you remember that?"

Robert nodded. "How bad?" he asked.

"You're going to be fine. You were brought in an ambulance to the hospital and you had emergency surgery for a severed brachial artery. You almost bled out, sir. You're a lucky guy. Surgeon said you probably won't even have much residual shoulder damage."

Robert lifted up the sheet. He was in a hospital gown but that was it. "Where are my pants?" he asked.

"I imagine they took them off you before surgery," the nurse said. "You didn't become my patient until you came to the recovery room. I can check for you."

"I need my pants," Robert said.

"They're not going to do you any good," the nurse said. "You're not going anywhere for a few days."

"Please. Can you just go look? I had a ring in my pocket. I was going to ask someone to marry me."

The young man smiled. "I got married last summer," he said. "I'll go look. Just don't try to get out of bed on me, okay?"

He wasn't going anywhere. He wiggled his fingers, grateful that he still could.

Severed brachial artery. That explained it. One minute he'd been standing, then his vision had grayed, and he'd realized he was going down for the count.

He needed to talk to Carmen. She might never be able to forgive him but he had to know for sure that she and Raoul were okay.

The door opened a few minutes later and he expected to see the nurse. But it was Carmen with her silky-shiny hair and her beautiful face peeking around the corner. "Hi," she said.

He tried to sit up in bed.

"No," she said gently. "Be still. I just talked to the doctor. You've lost a lot of blood. By the way, your mother is here. She's been entertaining everyone in the waiting room."

He shook his head.

"She's lovely," Carmen said.

"Are you okay? Raoul?"

She leaned down and brushed a kiss across his cheek. "We are both fine. We wouldn't be, you know, if you'd been even a minute later. That man was about to cut Raoul's fingers off. I've never been so frightened in my life. He said that I had to watch, that that was my punishment."

"Oh, honey," he said. He swallowed hard. "I'm so sorry you had to go through that."

"You saved our lives, Robert. You're making a habit of that." She rubbed her hand across the blankets. "Raoul told me about Speedy's Used Cars. He shot those car windshields out. That monster was with him."

He licked his dry lips. "I should have said something. I didn't have any proof but I did have my suspicions. I guess I didn't want to burn Raoul. Subconsciously, I think I didn't push as hard as I might have because I wanted Raoul to trust me, to like me." He hesitated. "I knew his opinion about me would matter to you."

"I was so angry," she said softly. "So hurt."

"I'm sorry," he said. It was inadequate but the best he could do. "I screwed up." Robert used his good arm and rubbed the back of his palm against his forehead. He had a bitch of a headache.

"There's something I need to tell you," she said.

Could he bear it? He nodded.

"I had some time to think," she said, "while you were fighting for your life. It's amazing what something like that does for perspective. I love you, Robert. I want you to know that."

He could feel his heart start to beat fast and figured he was ten seconds away from the alarm on some machine starting to wail. "But—"

The door opened. The nurse stuck his head around the corner. "Sorry, sir. Pants weren't where I thought they'd be. It's possible your personal belongings were already sent up to a room. I'm checking now," he said. He pulled back and the door closed.

His ring was MIA. That wasn't stopping him.

"Carmen, this is totally the wrong place and the wrong time but I waited once before to ask you this question and I'm not going to make that mistake again. I love you, too. I want to help you raise Raoul. I want us to be a family." He took a breath. "I can't promise that I won't make any more mistakes, but I can promise that every day I'll be thankful that you and Raoul are in my life and I'll work hard to always earn your trust and your love."

She didn't say anything, but her dark brown eyes were big.

"I had a ring in my pants pocket that I've been carrying around for days but apparently I've managed to lose it," he said. "And I'm afraid getting down on one knee is out of the question. So I'm doing this all wrong."

She shook her head. Her eyes were shimmering with tears.

"You're doing it perfectly. Yes, yes. I will marry you." She raised her arm that had been at her side. In her hand was a plastic bag. He could see his shoes sticking out the end.

He grabbed the bag from her. With one arm, he pulled everything out of the bag. When he got to the pants, he stuck his hand into the pocket.

It was there.

He pulled it out and flipped open the hinge of the silver box. "Be my wife, Carmen. I love you."

She slipped the ring onto her finger. It fit perfectly. His heart soared.

"I love you, Robert."

It was amazing. A minute ago, a cannon going off couldn't have gotten him out of the bed. Now he felt as if he could run down the damn hallway. Carmen was going to be his wife. "Is Raoul here?"

She nodded. "Right outside."

"Can you get him? I want to tell him."

They were back within seconds. Carmen had her arm wrapped around the boy's shoulder.

"Raoul," Robert said, "I've got a question for you."

The boy nodded.

"Do you have any sheet music for the 'Wedding March'?"

The boy's dark eyes, the eyes that were so like his sister's, blinked fast. A grin broke across his face. "You guys are getting married?"

"Yes," Robert and Carmen spoke at the same time.

"How do you feel about that?" Carmen added.

"I think it's great. Really great." Raoul pulled his cell phone from his pocket. "I've got to call Jacob. He's going to bust a gut."

Epilogue

Carmen Jimenez and Robert Hanson were married three weeks later, on a sunny, yet chilly, February day. The bride wore a long white dress and the groom wore a black suit with his arm in a sling.

Raoul Jimenez played the trombone, accompanied by Jacob Minelli on the drums.

At the reception, the bride and groom danced the first dance, the second dance and the third dance together. At the end of the night, they took a limo to the airport, where they caught a flight to Jamaica. In his carry-on, the groom packed a travel-size container of spring soap. In her carry-on, the bride packed M&M'S and microwave popcorn.

While they were on their honeymoon, Raoul stayed with Liz and Sawyer Montgomery and worked at Speedy's Used Cars, making restitution for broken windshields.

* * * * *

LARGER-PRINT BOOKS!
GET 2 FREE LARGER-PRINT NOVELS PLUS
2 FREE GIFTS!

HARLEQUIN®

INTRIGUE®

BREATHTAKING ROMANTIC SUSPENSE

HILP13R

REQUEST YOUR FREE BOOKS!
2 FREE RIVETING INSPIRATIONAL NOVELS
PLUS 2 FREE MYSTERY GIFTS

Love Inspired®
SUSPENSE

YES! Please send me 2 FREE Love Inspired® Suspense novels and my 2 FREE mystery gifts (gifts are worth about $10). After receiving them, if I don't wish to receive any more books, I can return the shipping statement marked "cancel." If I don't cancel, I will receive 4 brand-new novels every month and be billed just $4.74 per book in the U.S. or $5.24 per book in Canada. That's a savings of at least 21% off the cover price. It's quite a bargain! Shipping and handling is just 50¢ per book in the U.S. and 75¢ per book in Canada.* I understand that accepting the 2 free books and gifts places me under no obligation to buy anything. I can always return a shipment and cancel at any time. Even if I never buy another book, the two free books and gifts are mine to keep forever.

123/323 IDN F5AN

Name	(PLEASE PRINT)
Address	Apt. #
City	State/Prov.	Zip/Postal Code

Signature (if under 18, a parent or guardian must sign)

Mail to the Harlequin® Reader Service:
IN U.S.A.: P.O. Box 1867, Buffalo, NY 14240-1867
IN CANADA: P.O. Box 609, Fort Erie, Ontario L2A 5X3

**Are you a current subscriber to Love Inspired Suspense books and want to receive the larger-print edition?
Call 1-800-873-8635 or visit www.ReaderService.com.**

* Terms and prices subject to change without notice. Prices do not include applicable taxes. Sales tax applicable in N.Y. Canadian residents will be charged applicable taxes. Offer not valid in Quebec. This offer is limited to one order per household. Not valid for current subscribers to Love Inspired Suspense books. All orders subject to credit approval. Credit or debit balances in a customer's account(s) may be offset by any other outstanding balance owed by or to the customer. Please allow 4 to 6 weeks for delivery. Offer available while quantities last.

Your Privacy—The Harlequin® Reader Service is committed to protecting your privacy. Our Privacy Policy is available online at www.ReaderService.com or upon request from the Harlequin Reader Service.
We make a portion of our mailing list available to reputable third parties that offer products we believe may interest you. If you prefer that we not exchange your name with third parties, or if you wish to clarify or modify your communication preferences, please visit us at www.ReaderService.com/consumerschoice or write to us at Harlequin Reader Service Preference Service, P.O. Box 9062, Buffalo, NY 14269. Include your complete name and address.

LISDIR13R

ReaderService.com

Manage your account online!

- Review your order history
- Manage your payments
- Update your address

> *We've designed
> the Harlequin® Reader Service
> website just for you.*

Enjoy all the features!

- Reader excerpts from any series
- Respond to mailings and special monthly offers
- Discover new series available to you
- Browse the Bonus Bucks catalog
- Share your feedback

Visit us at:
ReaderService.com